TOM CORBETT, SPACE CADET:

THE REVOLT ON VENUS

A NOVEL BY
CAREY ROCKWELL

WILLY LEY
TECHNICAL ADVISOR

ROCKET SCIENCE BOOKS
AN IMPRINT OF DEAD LETTER PRESS
WWW.DEADLETTERPRESS.COM

TOM CORBETT, SPACE CADET:
THE REVOLT ON VENUS

Published 2017 by
ROCKET SCIENCE BOOKS
An imprint of
DEAD LETTER PRESS
WWW.DEADLETTERPRESS.COM
BOX 134, NEW KENT, VIRGINIA 23124-0134

Originally published in 1954 by Grosset & Dunlap, New York; and by permission of Rockhill Radio. This edition is © 2017 by Tom English.

Cover illustration by George Wilson and the Rocket Science Engineering Department; original interior illustrations by Louis Glanzman. Introduction © Series Editor Tom English.

Printed in the United States of America

ISBN-10: 0-9966936-6-1
ISBN-13: 978-0-9966936-6-0

FIRST ROCKET SCIENCE EDITION: November 2017

TYRANTS AND TYRANNOS!

MOST FANS OF THE *TOM CORBETT, SPACE CADET* novels believe *The Revolt on Venus* to be the best book of the series. The novel certainly has much to recommend it, including the return of two series characters, hard-as-nails spaceman Major "Blast Off" Connel and the brilliant but irascible Professor Sykes. Then too, there's nonstop mystery and mayhem in the form of a secret organization bent on overthrowing the Solar Alliance, and a fierce battle to preserve interplanetary freedom and democracy that reaches from the steaming jungles of Venus to the freezing oceans of space; not to mention ... *dinosaurs!*

Dinosaurs? On Venus?

The idea now seems absurd, but for decades the notion of terrible lizards ruling the turf of the second planet from the sun seemed more than plausible. Depictions of a Venus populated by dinosaurs frequently crop up in numerous pulp SF stories appearing throughout the first half of the twentieth century.

The first example of such science fiction, however, may be Gustavus W. Pope's 1895 adventure *Journey to Venus.* Pope described a lush Venutian landscape inhabited by vicious, dinosaur-like creatures. What in the world was Pope thinking?

At one time, Venus was thought to have large bodies of water; perhaps even an atmospheric blanket of moisture similar to the one described in the Book of Genesis,[1] suggesting a green-house effect and conjuring images of a lush, water-rich Eden, as depicted in C. S. Lewis' 1943 SF novel *Perelandra.* Such a world would suggest a stable, tropical climate similar to that of earth's prehistoric times —so there just had to be dinosaurs, right?

---

[1] In Genesis 1:7 (NIV): "So God made the vault and separated the water under the vault from the water above it."

These assumptions were based on nothing more than the initial observations of the seventeenth-century Italian astronomer Galileo Galilei, who described Venus as featureless, when his telescope was unable to pierce the mysteries hidden beneath the dense clouds covering the planet's surface. Carl Sagan, in his science series *Cosmos,* further explains the reasoning for the cognitive leap from thick clouds to huge reptiles:

> "I can't see a thing on the surface of Venus. Why not? Because it's covered with a dense layer of clouds. Well, what are clouds made of? Water, of course. Therefore, Venus must have an awful lot of water on it. Therefore, the surface must be wet. Well, if the surface is wet, it's probably a swamp. If there's a swamp, there's ferns. If there's ferns, maybe there's even *dinosaurs.*"

The idea of *hunting* these creatures may have originated in a magazine "article" appearing in the March 1950 issue of *Coronet,* "Mr Smith Goes to Venus," which allegedly reports on vacations to the planet (in the year 2500), where visitors can hunt the biggest game in the solar system. The story included several Chesley Bonestell illustrations depicting brochures from the future touting "big game hunting" on Venus—an activity that lures the cadets back to Astro's native world—as well as a dinosaur zoo (below).

For readers in 1954, traveling through space and stalking dinosaurs in the jungles of Venus were wild flights of fantasy; as successful rocket launches into space and even commercial air travel were still in their infancy. But other elements in *The Revolt on Venus* hit closer to home. After defeating Hitler a decade earlier, and then dealing with the Cold War aftermath of WWII, fascist dictators, secret alliances, and violent insurrections appeared all too real for most Americans.

Fortunately, Tom Corbett and his pals are always there ... fighting injustice at home and among the stars ... grappling with tyrants and tyrannos ... rescuing us from the problems of our times ... yesterday, today and tomorrow.

Tom English
New Kent, VA

Tom Corbett, Space Cadet blasted across the airwaves in 1950, when CBS debuted the Rockhill Studios television series. The show ran for five seasons, during which it appeared on all four networks of the day. It also launched a successful newspaper strip, a radio show (as *Space Cadet*), and a series of Dell comic books, not to mention scores of LP records, lunch boxes, toys, promotional giveaways, and eight science fiction novels by Carey Rockwell (with an assist from rocketry expert and spaceflight advocate Willy Ley, who served as Technical Advisor to both the books and the television show).

THE **TOM CORBETT, SPACE CADET** SERIES

NOW AVAILABLE FROM ROCKET SCIENCE BOOKS:

STAND BY FOR MARS!
DANGER IN DEEP SPACE
ON THE TRAIL OF THE SPACE PIRATES
THE SPACE PIONEERS
THE REVOLT ON VENUS

FORTHCOMING FROM ROCKET SCIENCE BOOKS:

TREACHERY IN OUTER SPACE
SABOTAGE IN SPACE
THE ROBOT ROCKET

ENJOY EXCITING SCIENCE FICTION ADVENTURES IN THE SPIRIT OF TOM CORBETT, SPACE CADET— IN EVERY ISSUE OF BLACK INFINITY.

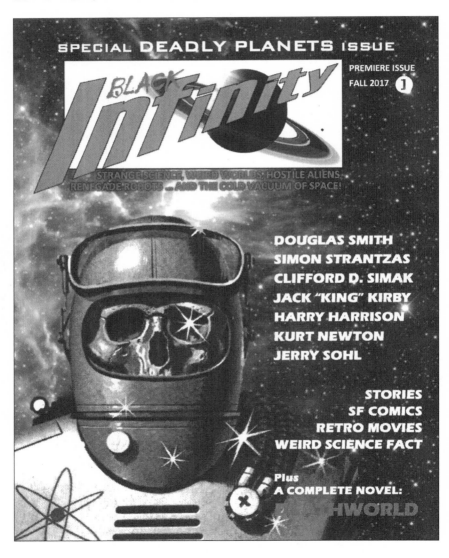

TOM CORBETT, SPACE CADET:

THE REVOLT ON VENUS

1 "EMERGENCY AIRLOCK OPEN!"

The tall, broad-shouldered officer, wearing the magnificent black-and-gold uniform of the Solar Guard, spoke into a small microphone and waited for an acknowledgment. It came almost immediately.

"Cadet Corbett ready for testing," a voice crackled thinly over the loud-speaker.

"Very well. Proceed."

Seated in front of the scanner screen on the control

deck of the rocket cruiser *Polaris,* Captain Steve Strong replaced the microphone in its slot and watched a bulky figure in a space suit step out of the airlock and drift away from the side of the ship. Behind him, five boys, all dressed in the vivid blue uniforms of the Space Cadet Corps, strained forward to watch the lone figure adjust the nozzles of the jet unit on the back of his space suit.

"Come on, Tom!" said the biggest of the five boys, his voice a low, powerful rumble as he rooted for his unit mate.

"If Tom makes this one," crowed the cadet next to him, a slender boy with a thick shock of close-cropped blond hair, "the *Polaris* unit is home free!"

"This is the last test, Manning," replied one of the remaining three cadets, the insigne of the *Arcturus* unit on the sleeve of his uniform. "*If* Corbett makes this one, you fellows deserve to win."

Aboard the rocket cruiser *Polaris,* blasting through the black void of space two hundred miles above Earth, six Space Cadets and a Solar Guard officer were conducting the final test for unit honors for the term. All other Academy units had been eliminated in open competition. Now, the results of the individual space orientation test would decide whether the three cadets of the *Arcturus* unit or the three cadets of the *Polaris* unit would win final top unit honors.

Roger Manning and Astro kept their eyes glued to the telescanner screen, watching their unit mate, Tom Corbett, drift slowly through space toward his starting position. The young cadet's task was basically simple; with his space helmet blacked out so that he could not see in any direction, he was to make his way back to the ship from a point a mile away, guided only by the audio orders from the examining officer aboard the ship. His score was measured by the time elapsed, and the amount of corrections and orders given by the examining officer. It was an exercise designed to test a cadet's steadiness under emergency conditions of space.

The three members of the *Arcturus* unit had completed their runs and had returned to the ship in excellent time. Roger and Astro had also taken their tests and now it depended on Tom. If he could return to the *Polaris* in less than ten minutes, with no more than three corrections, the *Polaris* unit would be victorious.

Seated directly in front of the scanner, Captain Steve Strong, the examining officer, watched the space-suited figure dwindle to a mere speck on the screen. As the regular skipper of the *Polaris* crew, he could not help secretly rooting for Tom, but he was determined to be fair, even to the extent of declaring the *Arcturus* unit the winner, should the decision be very close. He leaned forward to adjust the focus on the scanner, bringing the drifting figure into a close-up view, and then lifted the microphone to his lips.

"Stand by, Corbett!" he called. "You're getting close to range."

"Very well, sir," replied Tom. "Standing by."

Behind Strong, Roger and Astro looked at each other and turned back to the screen. As one, they crossed the fingers of both hands.

"Ready, Corbett!" called Strong. "You'll be clocked from the second you're on range. One hundred feet—seventy-five—fifty—twenty-five—ten—*time!*"

As the signal echoed in his blacked-out space helmet, Tom jerked his body around in a sudden violent move, and grasping the valve of the jet unit on his back, he opened it halfway. He waited, holding his breath, expecting to hear Captain Strong correct his course. He counted to ten slowly, and when no correction came over the headphones, he opened the valve wide and blindly shot through space.

Aboard the Polaris, Astro and Roger shouted with joy and Strong could not repress a grin. The tiny figure on the scanner was hurtling straight for the side of the *Polaris*!

As the image grew larger and larger, anxious eyes swiveled back and forth from the scanner screen to the steady sweeping hand of the chronometer. Roger bit his lip nervously, and Astro's hands trembled.

When Tom reached a point five hundred feet away from the ship, Strong flipped open the audio circuit and issued his first order.

"Range five hundred feet," he called. "Cut jets!"

"You're already here, spaceboy!" yelled Roger into the mike, leaning over Strong's shoulder. The captain silenced him with a glare. No one could speak to the examinee but the testing officer.

Tom closed the valve of his jet unit and blindly jerked himself around again to drift feet first toward the ship. Strong watched this approach closely, silently admiring the effortless way the cadet handled himself in weightless space. When Tom was fifty feet away from the ship, and still traveling quite fast, Strong gave the second order to break his speed. Tom opened the valve again and felt the tug of the jets braking his acceleration. He drifted slower and slower, and realizing that he was close to the hull of the ship, he stretched his legs, striving to make contact. Seconds later he felt a heavy thump at the soles of his feet, and within the ship there was the muffled clank of metal boot weights hitting the metal skin of the hull.

"Time!" roared Strong and glanced at the astral chronometer over his head. The boys crowded around as the Solar Guard captain quickly computed Tom's score. "Nine minutes, fifty-one seconds, and two corrections," he announced, unable to keep the pride out of his voice.

"We win! We win!" roared Roger. "Term honors go to the *Polaris!*"

Roger turned around and began pounding Astro on the chest, and the giant Venusian picked him up and waltzed him around the deck. The three members of the *Arcturus* unit waited until the first flush of victory died away and then crowded around the two boys to congratulate them.

"Don't forget the cadet who did it," commented Strong dryly, and the five cadets rushed below to the jet-boat deck to wait for Tom.

When Tom emerged from the airlock a few moments later, Roger and Astro swarmed all over him, and another wild dance began. Finally, shaking free of his well-meaning but violent unit mates, he grinned and gasped, "Well, from that reception, I guess I did it."

"Spaceboy"—Roger smiled—"you made the *Arcturus* unit look like three old men in a washtub counting toes!"

"Congratulations, Corbett," said Tony Richards of the *Arcturus* crew, offering his hand. "That was really fast maneuvering out there."

"Thanks, Tony." Tom grinned, running his hand through his brown curly hair. "But I have to admit I was a little scared. Wow! What a creepy feeling to know you're out in space alone and not able to see anything."

Their excitement was interrupted by Strong's voice over the ship's intercom. "Stand by, all stations!"

"Here we go!" shouted Roger. "Back to the Academy—and leave!"

"*Yeeeeooooow!*" Astro's bull-like roar echoed through the ship as the cadets hurried to their flight stations.

As command cadet of the *Polaris*, Tom climbed up to the control deck, and strapping himself into the command pilot's seat, prepared to get under way. Astro, the power-deck cadet who could "take apart a rocket engine and put it back together again with his thumbs," thundered below to the atomic rockets he loved more than anything else in the universe. Roger Manning, the third member of the famed *Polaris* unit, raced up the narrow ladder leading to the radar bridge to take command of astrogation and communications.

While Captain Strong and the members of the *Arcturus* unit strapped themselves into acceleration cushions, Tom conducted a routine check of the many gauges on the great control panel before him. Satisfied, he flipped open the intercom and called, "All stations, check in!"

"Radar deck, aye!" drawled Roger's lazy voice.

"Power deck, aye!" rumbled Astro.

"Energize the cooling pumps!" ordered Tom.

"Cooling pumps, aye!"

The whine of the mighty pumps was suddenly heard, moaning eerily throughout the ship.

"Feed reactant!"

The sharp hiss of fuel being forced into the rocket engines rose above the whine of the pumps, and the ship trembled.

"Stand by to blast," called Tom. "Standard space speed!"

Instantly the *Polaris* shot toward Earth in a long, curving arc. Moments later, when the huge round ball of the mother planet loomed large on the scanner screen, Roger's voice reported over the intercom, "Academy spaceport control gives us approach orbit 074 for touchdown on Ramp Twelve, Tom."

"074 Ramp Twelve," repeated Tom. "Got it!"

"Twelve!" roared Astro suddenly over the intercom. "Couldn't you make it closer to the Academy than that, Manning? We'll have to walk two miles to the nearest slidewalk!"

"Too bad, Astro," retorted Roger, "but I guess if I had to carry around as much useless muscle and bone as you do, I'd complain too!"

"I'm just not as lucky as you, Manning," snapped Astro quickly. "I don't have all that space gas to float me around."

"Knock it off, fellows," interjected Tom firmly. "We're going into our approach."

Lying on his acceleration cushion, Strong looked over at Tony Richards of the *Arcturus* unit and winked. Richards winked and smiled back. "They never stop, do they, sir?"

"When they do," replied Strong, "I'll send all three of them to sick bay for examination."

"Two hundred thousand feet to Earth's surface," called Tom. "Stand by for landing operations."

As Tom adjusted the many controls on the complicated operations panel of the ship, Roger and Astro followed his orders quickly and exactly. "Cut main drive rockets and give me one-half thrust on forward braking rockets!" ordered Tom, his eyes glued to the altimeter.

The *Polaris* shuddered under the sudden reverse in power, then began an upward curve, nose pointing back toward space. Tom barked another command. "Braking rockets full! Stand by main drive rockets!"

The sleek ship began to settle tailfirst toward its destination—Space Academy, U.S.A.

In the heart of a great expanse of cleared land in the western part of the North American continent, the cluster of buildings that marked Space Academy gleamed brightly in the noon sun. Towering over the green grassy quadrangle of the Academy was the magnificent Tower of Galileo, built of pure Titan crystal which gleamed like a gigantic diamond. With smaller buildings, including the study halls, the nucleonics laboratory, the cadet dormitories, mess halls, recreation halls, all connected by rolling slidewalks—and to the north, the vast area of the spaceport with its blast-pitted ramps—the Academy was the goal of every boy in the year A.D. 2353, the age of the conquest of space.

Founded over a hundred years before, Space Academy trained the youth of the Solar Alliance for service in the Solar Guard, the powerful force created to protect the liberties of the planets. But from the beginning, Academy standards were so high, requirements so strict, that not many made it. Of the one thousand boys enrolled every year, it was expected that only twenty-one of them would become officers, and of this group, only seven would be command pilots. The great Solar Guard fleet that patrolled the space lanes across the millions of miles between the satellites and planets possessed the finest, yet most complicated, equipment in the Alliance. To be an officer in the fleet required a combination of skills and technical knowledge so demanding that eighty percent of the Solar Guard officers retired at the age of forty.

High over the spaceport, the three cadets of the *Polaris* unit, happy over the prospect of a full month of freedom, concentrated on the task of landing the great ship on the Academy spaceport. Watching the teleceiver screen that gave him a view of the spaceport astern of the ship, Tom called into the intercom, "One thousand feet to touchdown. Cut braking rockets. Main drive full!"

The thunderous blast of the rockets was his answer, building up into roaring violence. Shuddering, the great cruiser eased to the ground foot by foot, perfectly balanced on the fiery exhaust from her main tubes.

Seconds later the giant shock absorbers crunched on the ramp and Tom closed the master switch cutting all power. He glanced at the astral chronometer over his head and then turned to speak into the audio log recorder. "Rocket cruiser *Polaris* completed space flight one-seven-six at 1301."

Captain Strong stepped up to Tom and clapped him on the shoulder. "Secure the *Polaris*, Tom, and tell Astro to get the reactant pile from the firing chamber ready for dumping when the hot-soup wagon gets here." The Solar

Guard officer referred to the lead-lined jet sled that removed the reactant piles from all ships that were to be laid up for longer than three days. "And you'd better get over to your dorm right away," Strong continued. "You have to get ready for parade and full Corps dismissal."

Tom grinned. "Yes, sir!"

"We're blasting off, sir," said Tony Richards, stepping forward with his unit mates. "Congratulations again, Corbett. I still can't figure out how you did it so quickly!"

"Thanks, Tony," replied Tom graciously. "It was luck and the pressure of good competition."

Richards shook hands and then turned to Strong. "Do I have your permission to leave the ship, sir?" he asked.

"Permission granted," replied Strong. "And have a good leave."

"Thank you, sir."

The three *Arcturus* cadets saluted and left the ship. A moment later Roger and Astro joined Strong and Tom on the control deck.

"Well," said Strong, "what nonsense have you three planned for your leave? Try and see Liddy Tamal. I hear she's making a new stereo about the Solar Guard. You might be hired as technical assistants." He smiled. The famous actress was a favorite of the cadets. Strong waited. "Well, is it a secret?"

"It was your idea, Astro," said Roger. "Go ahead."

"Yeah," said Tom. "You got us into this."

"Well, sir," mumbled Astro, turning red with embarrassment, "we're going to Venus."

"What's so unusual about going to Venus?" asked Strong.

"We're going hunting," replied Astro.

"Hunting?"

"Yes, sir," gulped the big Venusian. "For tyrannosaurus."

Strong's jaw dropped and he sat down suddenly on the nearest acceleration cushion. "I expected something a little strange from you three whiz kids." He laughed. "It would be impossible for you to go home and relax for a month. But this blasts me! Hunting for a tyrannosaurus! What are you going to do with it after you catch it?" He paused and then added, "If you do."

"Eat it," said Astro simply. "Tyrannosaurus steak is delicious!"

Strong doubled with laughter at the seriousness of Astro's expression. The giant Venusian continued doggedly, "And besides, there's a bounty on them. A thousand credits for every tyranno head brought in. They're dangerous and destroy a lot of crops."

Strong straightened up. "All right, all right! Go ahead! Have yourselves a good time, but don't take any unnecessary chances. I like my cadets to have all the arms and legs and heads they're supposed to have." He paused and glanced at his watch. "You'd better get hopping. Astro, did you get the pile ready for the soup wagon?"

"Yes, sir!"

"Very well, Tom, secure the ship." He came to attention. "Unit, *stand—to!*"

The three cadets stiffened and saluted sharply.

"Unit dismissed!"

Captain Strong turned and left the ship.

Hurriedly, Tom, Roger, and Astro checked the great spaceship and fifteen minutes later were racing out of the main airlock. Hitching a ride on a jet sled to the nearest slidewalk, they were soon being whisked along toward their quarters. Already, cadet units were standing around in fresh blues waiting for the call for final dress parade.

At exactly fifteen hundred, the entire Cadet Corps stepped off with electronic precision for the final drill of the term. By threes, each unit marching together, with the *Polaris* unit walking behind the standard bearers as honor unit, they passed the reviewing stand. Senior officers of the Solar Guard, delegates from the Solar Alliance, and staff officers of the Academy accepted their salute. Commander Walters stood stiffly in front of the stand, his heart filled with pride as he recognized the honor unit. He had almost washed out the *Polaris* unit in the beginning of their Academy training.

Major Lou Connel, Senior Line Officer of the Solar Guard, stepped forward when the cadets came to a stop and presented Tom, Roger, and Astro with the emblem of their achievement, a small gold pin in the shape of a rocket ship. He, too, had had his difficulties with the *Polaris* unit,† and while he had never been heard to compliment anyone on anything, expecting nothing but the best all the time, he nevertheless congratulated them heartily as he gave them their hard-won trophy.

After several other awards had been presented, Commander Walters addressed the Cadet Corps, concluding with "...each of you has had a tough year. But when you come back in four weeks, you'll think this past term has been a picnic. And remember, wherever you go, whatever you do, you're Space Cadets! Act like one! But above all, have a good time! Spaceman's luck!"

A cadet stepped forward quickly, turned to face the line of cadets, and held up his hands. He brought them down quickly and words of the Academy song thundered from a thousand voices.

> *From the rocket fields of the Academy*
> *To the far-flung stars of outer space,*
> *We're Space Cadets training to be*
> *Ready for dangers we may face.*
> *Up in the sky, rocketing past,*
> *Higher than high, faster than fast,*
> *Out into space, into the sun,*
> *Look at her go when we give her the gun.*
> *We are Space Cadets, and we are proud to say*
> *Our fight for right will never cease.*
> *Like a cosmic ray, we light the way*
> *To interplanet peace!*

"*Dis*-missed!" roared Walters. Immediately the precise lines of cadets turned into a howling mob of eager boys, everyone seemingly running in a different direction.

"Come on," said Roger. "I've got everything set! Let's get to the station ahead of the mob."

"But what about our gear?" said Tom. "We've got to get back to the dorm."

---

† The cadets briefly served under Major "Blast-Off" Connel, during a special mission to Alpha Centauri, in the second Tom Corbett novel, *Danger in Deep Space.*

"I had it sent down to the station last night. I got the monorail tickets to Atom City last week, and reserved seats on the *Venus Lark* two weeks ago! Come on!"

"Only Roger could handle it so sweetly," sighed Astro. "You know, hotshot, sometimes I think you're useful!"

The three cadets turned and raced across the quadrangle for the nearest slidewalk that would take them to the Academy monorail station and the beginning of their adventure in the jungles of Venus.

2 "THE SITUATION MAY BE SERIOUS AND IT MAY NOT, BUT I DON'T WANT TO TAKE ANY CHANCES."

Commander Walters sat in his office, high up in the Tower of Galileo, with department heads from the Academy and Solar Guard. Behind him, an entire wall made of clear crystal offered a breath-taking view of the Academy grounds. Before him, their faces showing their concern over a report Walters had just read, Captain Strong, Major Connel, Dr. Joan Dale, and Professor Sykes waited for the commanding officer of the Academy to continue.

"As you know," said Walters, "the resolution passed by the Council in establishing the Solar Guard specifically states that it shall be the duty of the Solar Guard to investigate and secure evidence for the Solar Alliance Council of any acts by any person, or group of persons, suspected of overt action against the Solar Constitution or the Universal Bill of Rights. Now, based on the report I've just read to you, I would like an opinion from each of you."

"For what purpose, Commander?" asked Joan Dale, the young and pretty astrophysicist.

"To decide whether it would be advisable to have a full and open investigation of this information from the Solar Guard attaché on Venus."

"Why waste time talking?" snapped Professor Sykes, the

chief of the nucleonics laboratory. "Let's investigate. That report sounds serious."

Major Connel leveled a beady eye on the little gray-haired man.

"Professor Sykes, an investigation is serious. When it is based on a report like this one, it is doubly serious, and needs straight and careful thinking. We don't want to hurt innocent people."

Sykes shifted around in his chair and glared at the burly Solar Guard officer. "Don't try to tell me anything about straight thinking, Connel. I know more about the Solar Constitution and the rights of our citizens than you'll know in ten thousand light years!"

"Yeah?" roared Connel. "And with all your brains you'd probably find out these people are nothing more than a harmless bunch of colonists out on a picnic!"

The professor shot out of his chair and waved an angry finger under Connel's nose. "And that would be a lot more than I'm finding out right now with that contraption of yours!" he shouted.

Connel's face turned red. "So that's how you feel about my invention!" he snapped.

"Yes, that's the way I feel about your invention!" replied Sykes hotly. "I know three cadets that could build that gadget in half the time it's taken you just to figure out the theory!"

Commander Walters, Captain Strong, and Joan Dale were fighting to keep from laughing at the hot exchange between the two veteran spacemen.

"They sound like the *Polaris* unit," Joan whispered to Strong.

Walters stood up. "Gentlemen! Please! We're here to discuss a report on the activities of a secret organization on Venus. I will have to ask you to keep to the subject at hand. Dr. Dale, do you have any comments on the report?" He turned to the young physicist who was choking off a laugh.

"Well, Commander," she began, still smiling, "the report is rather sketchy. I would like to see more information before any real decision is made."

Walters turned to Strong. "Steve?"

"I think Joan has the right idea, sir," he replied. "While the report indicates that a group of people on Venus are meeting regularly and secretly, and wearing some silly uniform, I think we need more information before ordering a full-scale investigation."

"He's right, Commander," Connel broke in. "You just can't walk into an outfit and demand a look at their records, books, and membership index, unless you're pretty sure you'll find something."

"Send a man from here," Strong suggested. "If you use anyone out of the Venus office, he might be recognized."

"Good idea," commented Sykes.

Joan nodded. "Sounds reasonable."

"How do you feel about it, Connel?" asked Walters.

Connel, still furious over Sykes's comment on his spectrum recorder, shot an angry glance at the professor. "I think it's fine," he said bluntly. "Who're you going to send?"

Walters paused before answering. He glanced at Strong and then back at Connel. "What about yourself?"

"Me?"

"Why not?" continued Walters. "You know as much about Venus as anyone, and you have a lot of friends there you can trust. Nose around a while, see what you can learn, unofficially."

"But what about my work on the spectrum recorder?" asked Connel.

"That!" snorted Sykes derisively. "Huh, that can be completed any time you want to listen to some plain facts about—"

"I'll never listen to anything you have to say, you dried-up old neutron chaser!" blasted Connel.

"Of course not," cackled Sykes. "And it's the same bullheaded stubbornness that'll keep you from finishing that recorder."

"I'm sorry, gentlemen," said Walters firmly. "I cannot allow personal discussions to interfere with the problem at hand. How about it, Connel? Will you go to Venus?"

Lou Connel was the oldest line officer in the Solar Guard, having recommended the slightly younger Walters for the post of commandant of Space Academy and the Solar Guard so that he himself could escape a desk job and continue blasting through space where he had devoted his entire life. While Walters had the authority to order him to accept the assignment, Connel knew that if he begged off because of his work on the recorder, Walters would understand and offer the assignment to Strong. He paused and then growled, "When do I blast off?"

Walters smiled and answered, "As soon as we contact Venus headquarters and tell them to expect you."

"Wouldn't it be better to let me go without any fanfare?" mused the burly spaceman. "I could just take a ship and act as though I'm on some kind of special detail. As a matter of fact, Higgleston at the Venusport lab has some information I could use."

"Anything Higgleston could tell you," interjected Sykes, "I can tell you! You're just too stubborn to listen to me."

Connel opened his mouth to blast the professor in return, but he caught a sharp look from Walters and he clamped his lips together tightly.

"I guess that's it, then," said Walters. "Anyone have any other ideas?" He glanced around the room. "Joan? Steve?"

Dr. Dale and Captain Strong shook their heads silently. Strong was disappointed that he had not been given the assignment on Venus. Four weeks at the deserted Academy would seem like living in a graveyard. Walters sensed his feelings, and smiling, he said, "You've been going like a hot rocket this past year, Steve. I have a specific assignment for you."

"Yes, sir!" Strong looked up eagerly.

"I want you to go to the Sweet Water Lakes around New Chicago—"

"Yes, sir?"

"—go to my cabin—"

"Sir?"

"—and go fishing!"

Strong grinned. "Thanks, skipper," he said quietly. "I guess I could use a little relaxation. I was almost tempted to join Corbett, Manning, and Astro. They're going hunting in the jungle belt of Venus for a tyrannosaurus!"

"Blast my jets!" roared Connel. "Those boys haven't killed themselves in the line of duty, so they go out and tangle with the biggest and most dangerous monster in the entire solar system!"

"Well," said Joan with a smile, "I'll put my money on Astro against a tyranno any time, pound for pound!"

"Hear, hear!" chimed in Sykes, and forgetting his argument with Connel, he turned to the spaceman. "Say, Lou," he said, "when you get to Venus tell Higgy I said to show you that magnetic ionoscope he's rigging up. It might give you some ideas."

"Thanks," replied Connel, also forgetting the hot exchange of a few minutes before. He stood up. "I'll take the *Polaris*, Commander. She's the fastest ship available with automatic controls for a solo hop."

"She's been stripped of her reactant pile, Major," said Strong. "It'll take a good eighteen hours to soup her up again."

"I'll take care of it," said Connel. "Are there any specific orders, Commander?"

"Use your own judgment, Lou," said Walters. "You know what we want and how far to go to get it. If you learn anything, we'll start a full-scale investigation. If not, we'll forget the whole matter and no one will get hurt."

"And the Solar Guard won't get a reputation of being nosy," added Strong.

Connel nodded. "I'll take care of it." He shook hands all around, coming to Sykes last. "Sorry I lost my temper, Professor," he said gruffly.

"Forget it, Major." Sykes smiled. He really admired the gruff spaceman.

The thick-set senior officer came to smart attention, saluted crisply, turned, and left the office. For the time being, the mysterious trouble on Venus was his responsibility.

"ATOM CITY EXPRESS LEAVING ON TRACK FOUR!"

A metallic voice boomed over the station loud-speaker, as last-minute passengers boarded the long line of gleaming white monorail cars, hanging from a single overhead steel rail. In the open doorway of one of the end cars, a conductor lifted his arm, then paused and waited patiently as three Space Cadets raced down the stairs and along the platform in a headlong dash for the train. They piled inside, almost one on top of the other.

"Thanks for waiting, sir," gasped Tom Corbett.

"Not at all, Cadet," said the conductor. "I couldn't let you waste your leave waiting for another train."

The elderly man flipped a switch in the narrow vestibule and the door closed with a soft hiss of air. He inserted a light key into a nearby socket and twisted it gently, completing a circuit that flashed the "go" light in the engineer's cab. Almost immediately, the monorail train eased forward, suspended on the overhead rail. By the time the last building of Space Academy flashed past, the train was rolling along at full speed on its dash across the plains to Atom City.

The ride to the great metropolis of the North American continent was filled with excitement and anticipation for the three members of the *Polaris* crew. The cars were crowded with cadets on leave, and while there was a lot of joking and horseplay, the few civilian passengers were impressed with the gentlemanly bearing of the young spacemen. Tom and Roger finally settled down to read the latest magazines supplied by the monorail company. But Astro headed for the dining car where he attracted a great deal of attention by his order of a dozen eggs, followed by two orders of waffles and a full quart of milk. Finally, when the dining-car steward called a halt, because it was closing time, Astro made his way back to Tom and Roger with a plastic bag of French fried potatoes, and the three boys sat, munching them happily. The countryside flashed by in a blur of summer color as the train roared on at a speed of two hundred miles an hour.

A few hours and four bags of potatoes later, Astro yawned and stretched his enormous arms, nearly poking Roger in the eye.

"Hey, ya big ape!" growled Roger. "Watch the eye!"

"You'd never miss it, Manning," said Astro. "Just use your radar."

"Never mind, I like this eye just the way it is."

"We're almost there," called Tom. He pointed out the

crystal window and they could see the high peaks of the Rocky Mountain range looming ahead. "We cut through the new tunnel in those mountains and we'll be in Atom City in ten minutes!"

There was a bustle of activity around them as other cadets roused themselves and collected their gear. Once again conversation became animated and excited as the train neared its destination. Flashing into the tunnel, the line of cars began to slow down, rocking gently.

"We'd better go right out to the spaceport," said Tom, pulling his gear out of the recessed rack under his seat. "Our ship blasts off for Venus in less than a half-hour."

"Boy, it'll be a pleasure to ride a spaceship without having to astrogate," said Roger. "I'll just sit back and take it easy. Hope there are some good-looking space dolls aboard."

Tom turned to Astro. "You know, Astro," he said seriously, "it's a good thing we're along to take care of this Romeo. If he were alone, he'd wind up in another kind of hunt."

"I'd like to see how Manning's tactics work on a female *dasypus novemcinctur maximus*," said Astro with a sly grin.

"A female what?" yelled Roger.

"A giant armadillo, Roger," Tom explained, laughing. "Very big and very mean when they don't like you. Don't forget, everything on Venus grows big because of the lighter gravity."

"Yeah," drawled Roger, looking at Astro. "Big and dumb!"

"What was that again?" bellowed the giant Venusian, reaching for the flip cadet. The next moment, Roger was struggling futilely, feet kicking wildly as Astro held him at arm's length six inches off the floor. The cadets in the car roared with laughter.

"Atom City!" a voice over the intercar communicator boomed and the boys looked out the window to see the towering buildings of Atom City slowly slide by. The train had scarcely reached a full stop when the three cadets piled out of the door, raced up the slidestairs, and jumped into a jet cab. Fifteen minutes later they marched up to one of the many ticket counters of the Atom City Interplanetary Spaceport.

"Reservations for Cadets Corbett, Manning, and Astro on the *Venus Lark*, please," announced Tom.

The girl behind the counter ran her finger down a passenger manifest, nodded, and then suddenly frowned. She turned back to Tom and said, "I'm sorry, Cadet, but your reservations have been pre-empted by a priority listing."

"Priority!" roared Roger. "But I made those reservations two weeks ago. If there was a change, why didn't you tell us before?"

"I'm sorry, sir," said the girl patiently, "but according to the manifest, the priority call just came in a few hours ago. Someone contacted Space Academy, but you had already left."

"Well, is there another ship for Venusport today?"

"Yes," she replied and picked up another manifest. Glancing at it quickly, she shook her head. "There are no open reservations," she said. "I'm afraid the next flight for Venusport with open reservations isn't for four days."

"Blast my jets!" growled Roger disgustedly. "Four days!" He sat down on his gear and scowled. Astro leaned against the desk and stared gloomily at the floor. At that moment a young man with a thin face and a strained intense look pushed Tom to one side with a curt "Excuse me!" and stepped up to the desk.

"You're holding three reservations on the *Venus Lark*," he spoke quickly. "Priority number four-seven-six, S.D."

Tom, Roger, and Astro looked at him closely. They saw him nervously pay for his tickets and then walk away quickly without another look at the ticket girl.

"Were those our seats, miss?" asked Tom.

The girl nodded.

The three cadets stared after the young man who had bumped them off their ship.

"The symbol S.D. on the priority stands for Solar Delegate," said Roger. "Maybe he's a messenger."

The young man was joined by two other men also dressed in Venusian clothing, and after a few words, they all turned and stepped onto the slidewalk rolling out to the giant passenger ship preparing to blast off.

"This is the most rocket-blasting bit of luck in the universe!" growled Roger. "Four days!"

"Cheer up, Roger," said Tom. "We can spend the four days in Atom City. Maybe Liddy Tamal is here. We can follow Captain Strong's suggestion."

"Even she doesn't make four days delay sound exciting," interrupted Roger. "Come on. We might as well go back to town or we won't even get a room."

He picked up his gear and walked back to the jet cabstand. Astro and Tom followed the blond-haired cadet glumly.

The stand was empty, but a jet cab was just pulling up to the platform with a passenger. As the boys walked over to wait at the door, it opened and a familiar figure in a black-and-gold uniform stepped out.

"Captain Strong!"

"Corbett!" exclaimed Strong. "What are you doing here? I thought you were aboard the *Venus Lark*."

"We were bumped out of our reservation by an S.D. priority," said Astro.

"And we can't get out of here for another four days," added Roger glumly.

Strong sympathized. "That's rough, Astro." He looked at the three dour faces and then said, "Would you consider getting a free ride to Venus?"

The three cadets looked up hopefully.

"Major Connel's taking the *Polaris* to Venus to complete some work with Professor Higgleston in the Venus lab," explained Strong. "If you can get back to the Academy before he blasts off, he might give you a ride."

"No, thanks!" said Roger. "I'd rather sit here."

"Wait a minute, Roger," said Tom. "We're on leave, remember? And it's only a short hop to Venus."

"Yeah, hotshot," added Astro. "We'll get to Venus faster than the *Venus Lark*, and save money besides."

"OK," said Roger. "I guess I can take him for a little while."

Strong suppressed a smile. Roger's reluctance to go with Connel was well founded. Any cadet within hailing distance of the hard-bitten spaceman was likely to wind up with a bookful of demerits.

"Are you on an assignment, sir?" asked Tom.

"Vacation," said Strong. "Four weeks of fishing at Commander Walters' cabin at Sweet Water Lakes."

"If you pass through New Chicago," said Tom, "you would be welcome to stop in at my house. Mom and Dad would be mighty happy to meet you. And I think Billy, my kid brother, would flip a rocket."

"Thank you, Tom. I might do that if I have time." He looked at his watch. "You three had better hurry. I'd advise taking a jetcopter back to the Academy. You might not make it if you wait for a monorail."

"We'll do that, sir," said Tom.

The three boys threw their gear into the waiting cab and piled in. Strong watched them roar away, frowning in thought. An S.D. priority, the highest priority in space, was used only by special couriers on important missions for one of the dele-gates. He shrugged it off. "Getting to be as suspicious as an old space hen," he said to himself. "Fishing is what I need. A good fight with a trout in-stead of a space con-spiracy!"

3 "BLAST OFF—MINUS—FIVE—FOUR—THREE—TWO—ONE—*ZERO!*"

As the main drive rockets blasted into life, Tom fell back in his seat before the control panel of the *Polaris* and felt the growing thrust as the giant ship lifted off the ground, accelerating rapidly. He kept his eyes on the tele-ceiver screen and saw Space Academy fall away behind them. On the power deck Astro lay strapped in his accel-eration cushion, his outstretched hand on the emergency booster rocket switch should the main rockets fail before the ship could reach the free fall of space. On the radar bridge Roger watched the far-flung stars become brighter as the rocket ship hurtled through the dulling layers of the atmosphere.

As soon as the ship reached weightless space, Tom flipped on the gravity generators and put the *Polaris* on her course to Venus. Almost immediately the intercom began to blast.

"Now hear this!" Major Connel's voice roared. "Corbett, Manning, and Astro! I don't want any of your space-blasted nonsense on this trip! Get this ship to Venusport in the shortest possible time without burning out the pump bearings. And, Manning—!"

"Yes, sir," replied the blond-haired cadet.

"If I so much as hear one wisecrack between you and that overgrown rocket jockey, Astro, I'll log both of you twenty-five demerits!"

"I understand, sir," acknowledged Roger lazily. "I rather appreciate your relieving me of the necessity of speaking to that space ape!"

Listening to their voices on the control deck, Tom grinned and waited expectantly. He wasn't disappointed.

"Ape?" came a bull-like roar from the power deck. "Why, you skinny moth-eaten piece of space junk—"

"Cadet Astro!"

"Yes, sir?" Astro was suddenly meek.

"If you say one more word, I'll bury you in demerits!"

"But, sir—"

"No *buts*!" roared Connel. "And you, Manning—!"

"Yes, sir?" chimed in Roger innocently.

"Keep your mouth shut!"

"Very well, sir," said Roger.

"Corbett?"

"Yes, sir?"

"I'm putting you in charge of monitoring the intercom. If those two space idiots start jabbering again, call me. That's an order! I'll be in my quarters working." Connel switched off abruptly.

"You hear that, fellows?" said Tom. "Knock it off."

"OK, Tom," replied Roger, "just keep him out of my sight."

"That goes for me, too," added Astro. "Ape! Just wait till I—"

"Astro!" Tom interrupted sharply.

"OK, OK," groaned the big cadet.

Glancing over the panel once more and satisfying himself that the ship was functioning smoothly, Tom sighed and settled back in his seat, enjoying the temporary peace and solitude. It had been a tough year, filled with intensive study in the quest for an officer's commission in the Solar Guard. Space Academy was the finest school in the world, but it was also the toughest.

The young cadet shook his head, remembering a six-weeks' grind he, Roger, and Astro had gone through on a nuclear project. Knowing how to operate an atomic rocket motor was one thing, but understanding what went on inside the reactant pile was something else entirely. Never had the three cadets worked harder, or more closely together. But Astro's thorough, practical knowledge of basic nucleonics, combined with Roger's native wizardry at higher mathematics, and his own understanding of the theory, had enabled them to pull through with a grade of seventy-two, the highest average ever made by a cadet unit not specializing in physics.

As the ship rocketed smoothly through the airless void of space toward the misty planet of Venus, Tom made another quick but thorough check of the panel, and then returned to his reflections on the past term. It had been particularly difficult since they had missed many valuable hours of classroom work and study because of their adventure on the new colony of Roald,‡ but they had come through somehow. He shook his head wondering how they had made it. Forty-two units had washed out during the term. Instead of getting easier, the courses of study were getting more difficult all the time, and in his speech on the parade grounds, Commander Walters had promised—

"Emergency!" Roger's voice over the intercom brought Tom out of his reverie sharply.

"All hands," continued the cadet on the radar bridge

---

‡ As described in the previous novel, *The Space Pioneers.*

hurriedly, "secure your stations and get to the jet-boat deck on the double! Emergency!"

As the sharp clang of the emergency alarm rang out, Tom did not stop to question Roger's sudden order. Neutralizing all controls, he leaped for the hatch leading below. Taking the ladder four steps at a time, Tom saw Major Connel tear out of his quarters. The elder spaceman dived for the ladder himself, not stopping to ask questions. He was automatic in his reliance on the judgment of others. The few seconds spent in talk could mean the difference between life and death in space where you seldom got a second chance.

Tom and Connel arrived on the jet-boat deck to find Astro already preparing the small space craft for launching. As they struggled into space suits, Roger appeared. In answer to their questioning looks, he explained laconically, "Unidentifiable object attached to ship on fin parallel to steering vanes. Thought we'd better go outside first and examine later."

Connel nodded his mute agreement, and thirty seconds later the tiny jet boat was blasting out of the escape lock into space.

Circling around the ship to the stern, the jet boat, under Major Connel's sure touch, stopped fifty feet from the still glowing, exhaust tubes. He and the three cadets stared out at a small metallic boxlike object attached to the underside of the stabilizer fin.

"What do you suppose it is?" asked Astro.

"I don't know," replied Roger, "but it sure doesn't belong there. That's why I rang the emergency on you."

"You were absolutely right, Manning," asserted Connel. "If it's harmless, we can always get back aboard and nothing's been lost except a little time." He rose from the pilot's seat and stepped toward the hatch.

"Come with me, Corbett. We'll have a look. And bring the radiation counter along."

"Aye, aye, sir!"

Tom reached into a nearby locker, and pulling out a small, rectangular box with a round hornlike grid in its face, plunged out of the hatch with Major Connel and blasted across the fifty-foot gap to the stabilizer fin of the *Polaris.*

Connel gestured toward the object on the fin. "See if she's hot, Corbett."

The young cadet pressed a small button on the counter and turned the horn toward the mysterious box. Immediately the needle on the dial above the horn jumped from white to pink and finally red, quivering against the stop pin.

"Hot!" exclaimed Tom. "She almost kicked the pin off!"

"Get off the ship!" roared Connel. "It's a fission bomb with a time fuse!"

Tom dove at the box and tried to pull it off the stabilizer, but Major Connel grabbed him by the arm and wrenched him out into space.

"You space-blasted idiot!" Connel growled. "That thing's liable to go off any second! Get away from here!"

With a mighty shove, the spaceman sent Tom flying out toward the jet boat and then jumped to safety himself. Within seconds he and the young cadet were aboard the jet boat again and, not stopping to answer Astro's or Roger's questions, he jammed his foot down hard on the acceleration lever, sending the tiny ship blasting away from the *Polaris.*

Not until they were two miles away from the stricken rocket ship did Connel bring the craft to a stop. He turned and gazed helplessly at the gleaming hull of the *Polaris.*

"So they know," he said bitterly. "They're trying to stop me from even reaching Venus."

The three cadets looked at each other and then at the burly spaceman, bewilderment in their eyes.

"What's this all about, sir?" Roger finally asked.

"I'm not at liberty to tell you, Manning," replied Connel. "Though I want to thank you for your quick thinking. How

did you happen to discover the bomb?"

"I was sighting on Regulus for a position check and Regulus was dead astern, so when I swung the periscope scanner around, I spotted that thing stuck to the fin. I didn't bother to think about it, I just yelled."

"Glad you did," nodded Connel and turned to stare at the *Polaris* again. "Now I'm afraid we'll just have to wait until that bomb goes off."

"Isn't there anything we can do?" asked Tom.

"Not a blasted thing," replied Connel grimly. "Thank the universe we shut off all power. If that baby had blown while the reactant was feeding into the firing chambers, we'd have wound up a big splash of nothing."

"This way," commented Astro sourly, "it'll just blast a hole in the side of the ship."

"We might be able to repair that," said Tom hopefully.

"There she goes!" shouted Roger.

Staring out the windshield, they saw a sudden blinding flash of light appear over the stern section of the *Polaris*, a white-hot blaze of incandescence that made them flinch and crouch back.

"By the craters of Luna!" exclaimed Connel.

Before their eyes they saw the stabilizer fin melt and curl under the intense heat of the bomb. There was no sound or shock wave in the vacuum of space, but they all shuddered as though an overwhelming force had swept over them. Within seconds the flash was gone and the *Polaris* was drifting in the cold blackness of space! The only outward damage visible was the twisted stabilizer, but the boys realized that she must be a shambles within.

"I guess we'll have to wait a while before we go back

aboard. There might be radioactivity around the hull," Roger remarked.

"I don't think so," said Tom. "The *Polaris* was still coasting when we left her. We cut out the drive rockets, but we didn't brake her. She's probably drifted away from the radioactivity already."

"Corbett's right," said Connel. "A hot cloud would be a hundred miles away by now." He pressed down on the acceleration lever and the jet boat eased toward the ship. Edging cautiously toward the stern of the spaceship, they saw the blasted section of the fin already cooling in the intense cold of outer space.

"Think I'd better call a Solar Guard patrol ship, sir?" asked Roger.

"Let's wait until we check the damage, Manning," replied Connel.

"Yeah," chimed in Astro grimly, "if I can help it, I'm going to bring the *Polaris* in." He paused and then added, "If I have to carry her on my back."

As soon as a quick check with the radiation counter showed them that the hull was free of radioactivity, Major Connel and the three cadets re-entered the ship.

While the lack of atmosphere outside had dissipated the full force of the blast, the effect on the inside of the ship, where Earth's air pressure was maintained, was devastating. Whole banks of delicate machinery were torn from the walls and scattered over the decks. The precision instruments of the inner hull showed no signs of leakage, and the oxygen-circulating machinery could still function on an auxiliary power hookup.

Completing the quick survey of the ship, Major Connel realized that they would never be able to continue their flight to Venus and instructed Roger to contact the nearest Solar Guard patrol ship to pick them up.

"The *Polaris* will have to be left in space," continued Connel, "and a maintenance crew will be sent out to see if she can be repaired. If they decide it isn't worth the labor, they'll junk her here in space."

The faces of the three cadets fell.

"But there's no real damage on her power deck, sir," said

Astro. "And the hull is in good shape, except for the stabilizer fin and some of the stern plates. Why, sometimes a green Earthworm unit will crack a fin on their first touchdown."

"And the radar deck can be patched up easy, sir," spoke up Roger. "With some new tubes and a few rolls of wire I could have her back in shape in no time."

"That goes for the control deck, too!" said Tom doggedly. Then, after a quick glance at his unit mates, he faced Connel squarely. "I think it goes without saying, sir, that we'd appreciate it very much if you could recommend that she be restored instead of junked."

Connel allowed himself a smile in the face of such obvious love for the ship. "You forget that to repair her out in space, the parts have to be hauled from Venus. But I'll see what I can do. Meantime, Roger, see if you can't get that patrol ship to give us a lift to Venusport. Tell the C.O. I'm aboard and on urgent official business."

"Yes, sir," said Roger.

"And," continued the spaceman, noticing the downcast looks of Tom and Astro, "it wouldn't hurt if you two started repairing as much as you can. So when the maintenance crew arrives, they won't find her in such a mess."

"Yes, sir!" chorused the two cadets happily.

Connel returned to his quarters and sat down heavily in the remains of his bunk, rubbing his chin thoughtfully. Somehow, word had gotten out that he was going to check on the secret organization on Venus and someone had made a bold and desperate attempt to stop him before he could get started. It infuriated him to think that anyone would interrupt official business. As far as Connel was concerned, nothing came before official business. And he was doubly furious at the danger to the three cadets, who had innocently hitched a ride on what was almost a death ship. Someone was going to pay, Connel vowed, clenching his huge fists—and pay dearly.

4 *"YEEOOOWWW!"* Roaring with jubilation and jumping high in the air at every other step, Astro raced out of the gigantic maintenance hangar at the Venusport spaceport and charged at his two unit mates waiting on the concrete apron.

"Everything's OK," he yelled, throwing his arms around them. "The *Polaris* is going to be brought in for full repairs! I just saw the audiograph report from the maintenance chief!"

Tom and Roger broke into loud cheers and pounded each other on the back.

"Great Jupiter," gasped Roger, "I feel as though I've been sitting up with a sick friend!"

"Your friend's going to make a full recovery," asserted Astro.

"Did you see Major Connel?" asked Tom.

"Yeah," said Astro. "I think he had a lot to do with it. I saw him talking to the head maintenance officer."

"Well, now that we've sweated the old girl through the crisis," asserted Roger, "how's about us concentrating on our vacation?"

"Great," agreed Tom. "This is your party, Astro. Lead the way."

The three cadets left the spaceport in a jet cab and rode happily into the city of Venusport. As they slid along the superhighway toward the first and largest of the Venusian cities, Astro pointed out the sights. Like slim fingers of glass, the towering Titan crystal buildings of the city arose before them, reaching above the misty atmosphere to catch the sunlight.

"Where do we get our safari gear, Astro?" asked Roger.

"In the secondhand shops along Spaceman's Row," replied the big Venusian. "We can get good equipment down there at half the price."

The cab turned abruptly off the main highway and began twisting through a section of the city shunned by the average Venusian citizen. Spaceman's Row had a long and unsavory history. For ten square blocks it was the hideout and refuge of the underworld of space. The grimy stores and shadowy buildings supplied the needs of the countless shady figures who lived beyond the law and moved as silently as ghosts.

Leaving the jet cab, the three cadets walked along the streets, past the cheaply decorated storefronts and dingy hallways, until they finally came to a corner shop showing the universal symbol of the pawnshop: three golden balls. Tom and Roger looked at Astro who nodded, and they stepped inside.

The interior of the shop was filthy. Rusted and worn space gear was piled in heaps along the walls and on dusty counters. An old-fashioned multiple neon light fixture cast an eerie blue glow over everything. Roger grimaced as he looked around. "Are you sure we're in the right place, Astro?"

Tom winked. Roger had a reputation for being fastidious.

"This is it," nodded Astro. "I know the old geezer that runs this place. Nice guy. Name's Spike." He turned to the back of the shop and bawled, "Hey, Spike! Customers!"

Out of the gloomy darkness a figure emerged slowly. "Yeah?" The man stepped out into the pale light. He dragged one foot as he walked. "Whaddaya want?"

Astro looked puzzled. "Where's Spike?" he asked. "Doesn't Spike Freyer own this place?"

"He died a couple months ago. I bought him out just before." The crippled man eyed the three cadets warily. "Wanna buy something?"

Astro looked shocked. "Spike, dead? What happened?"

"How should I know," snarled the little man. "I bought him out and he died a few weeks later. Now, you wanna buy something or not?"

"We're looking for jungle gear," said Tom, puzzled by the man's strange belligerence.

"Jungle gear?" the man's eyes widened. "Going hunting?"

"Yeah," supplied Roger. "We need complete outfits for

three. But you don't look like you have them. Let's go, fellas." He turned toward the door, anxious to get out into the open air.

"Just a minute! Just a minute, Cadet," said the proprietor eagerly. "I've got some fine hunting gear here! A little used, but you won't mind that! Save you at least half on anything you'd buy up in the city." He started toward the back of the store and then paused. "Where you going hunting?"

"Why?" asked Tom.

"So I'll know what kind of gear you need. Light—heavy—kind of guns—"

"Jungle belt in the Eastern Hemisphere," supplied Astro.

"Big game?" asked the man.

"Yeah. Tyrannosaurus."

"Tyranno, eh?" nodded the little man. "Well, now, you'll need heavy stuff for that. I'd say at least three heavy-duty  paralo-ray pistols for sidearms, and three shock rifles. Then you'll need camping equipment, synthetics, and all the rest." He counted the items off on grubby little fingers.

"Let's take a look at the blasters," said Tom.

"Right this way," said the man. He turned and limped to the rear of the shop, followed by the three cadets. Opening a large cabinet, he pulled out a heavy rifle, a shock gun that could knock out any living thing at a range of a thousand yards, and stun the largest animal at twice the distance.

"This blaster will knock the scales off any tyranno that you hit," he said, handing the weapon over to Tom who expertly broke it down and examined it.

As Tom checked the gun, the proprietor turned to the other cadets casually.

"Why would three cadets want to go into that section of the jungle belt?"

"We just told you," said Roger. "We're hunting tyranno."

"Uh, yes, of course." He turned away and pulled three heavy-duty paralo-ray pistols out of the cabinet. "Now these ray-guns are the finest money can buy. Standard Solar Guard equipment...."

"Where did you get them?" demanded Roger sharply.

"Well, you know how it is, Cadet." The man laughed. "One way or another, we get a lot of gear. A man is discharged from the Solar Guard and he can keep his equipment, then he gets hard up for a few credits and so he comes to me."

Tom closed the shock rifle and turned to Astro. "This gun is clean enough. Think it can stop a tyranno, Astro?"

"Sure," said the big cadet confidently. "Easy."

"OK," announced Tom, turning back to the proprietor. "Give us the rest of the stuff."

"And watch your addition when you make out the bill," said Roger blandly. "We can add, too."

A half-hour later the three cadets stood in front of the shop with all the gear they would need and hailed a jet cab. They stowed their newly purchased equipment inside and started to climb in as Astro announced, "Spaceport, driver!"

"Huh?" Roger paused. "Why back there?"

"How do you think we're going to get to the jungle belt?" asked Astro. "Walk?"

"Well, no, but—"

"We have to rent a jet launch," said Astro. "Or try to buy a used one that we can sell back again. Pile in, now!"

As the cab shot away from the curb with the three cadets, the proprietor of the pawnshop stepped out of the doorway and watched it disappear, a puzzled frown on his face. Quickly he re-entered the shop, and limping to a small locker in the rear, opened it, exposing the screen of a teleceiver. He flipped on the switch, tuned it carefully, and in a moment the screen glowed to life.

"Hello, this is the shop," called the little man. "Lemme speak to Lactu! This is urgent!" As he waited he stared out through the dirty window to the street where the cadets had been a moment before and he smiled thinly.

ARRIVING AT THE SPACEPORT, Astro led his unit mates to a

privately owned repair hangar and dry dock where wealthier Venusian citizens kept their space yachts, jet-powered craft, and small runabouts. Astro opened the door to the office with a bang, and a young girl, operating an automatic typewriter, looked up.

"Astro!" she cried. "How wonderful to see you!"

"Hiya, Agnes," replied Astro shyly. The big cadet was well known and liked at the repair hangar. His early life had been spent in and around the spaceport. First just listening to the stories of the older spacemen and running errands for them, then lending a helping hand wherever he could, and finally becoming a rigger and mechanic. This all preceded his years as an enlisted spaceman and his eventual appointment to Space Academy. His big heart and honesty, his wild enthusiasm for any kind of rocket power had won him many friends.

"Is Mr. Keene around?" asked Astro.

"He's with a customer right now," replied Agnes. "He'll be out in a minute." Her eyes swept past Astro to Tom and Roger who were standing in the doorway. "Who are your friends?"

"Oh, excuse me!" mumbled Astro. "These are my unit mates, Cadet Corbett and Cadet Manning."

Before Tom could acknowledge the introduction, Roger stepped in front of him and sat on the edge of the desk. Looking into her eyes, he announced, "Tell you what, Astro, you and Tom go hunting. I've found all I could ever want to find right here. Tell me, my little space pet, are you engaged for dinner tonight?"

Agnes looked back into his eyes innocently. "As a matter of fact I am." Then, grinning mischievously, she added, "But don't let that stop you."

"I wouldn't let a tyranno stop me," bragged the blond-haired cadet. "Tell me who your previous engagement is with and I'll get rid of him in nothing flat!"

The girl giggled and looked past Roger. He turned to see a tall, solidly built man in coveralls scowling at him.

"Friend of yours, Agnes?" the newcomer asked.

"Friend of Astro's, Roy," said Agnes. "Cadet Manning, I'd like you to meet my brother, Roy Keene."

Roger jumped up and stuck out his hand. "Oh—er—ah—how do you do, sir?"

"Quite well, Cadet," replied Keene gruffly, but with a slight twinkle in his eye. He turned to Astro and gripped the big cadet's hand solidly. "Well, Astro, it's good to see you. How's everything going at Space Academy?"

"Swell, sir," replied Astro, and after introducing Tom and bringing Keene up to date on his life history, he explained the purpose of their visit. "We're on summer leave, sir, and we'd like to go hunting tyrannosaurus. But what we need most right now is a jet boat. We'd like to rent one, or if you've got something cheap, we'd buy it."

Keene rubbed his chin. "I'm afraid I can't help you, Astro. There's nothing available in the shop right now. I'd lend you my Beetle, but one of the boys has it out on a three-day repair job."

Astro's face fell. "Oh, that's too bad." He turned to Tom and Roger. "Well, we could drop in from a stratosphere cruiser and then work our way back to the nearest colony in three or four weeks."

"Wait a minute!" exclaimed Keene. "I've got an idea." He turned and called to a man standing on the other side of the hangar, studying a radar scanner for private yachts. "Hey, Rex, mind coming over here a minute."

The man walked over. He was in his late thirties, tall and broad-shouldered, his hair was almost snow-white, contrasting sharply with his deeply tanned and handsome features.

"This is the *Polaris* unit from Space Academy, Rex," said Keene. "Boys, meet Rex Sinclair." After the introductions were completed, Keene explained the cadets' situation. Sinclair broke into a smile. "It would be a pleasure to have you three boys as my guests!"

"Guests!" exclaimed Tom.

Sinclair nodded. "I have a plantation right on the edge of the jungle belt. Things get pretty dull down there in the middle of the summer. I'd be honored if you'd use my home as a base of operations while you hunt for your tyrannosaurus. As a matter of fact, you'd be helping me out. Those brutes destroy a lot of my crops and we have to go after them every three or four years."

"Well, thanks," said Tom, "but we wouldn't want to impose. We'd be happy to pay you—"

Sinclair held up his hand. "Wouldn't think of it. Do you have your gear?"

"Yes, sir," replied Astro. "Arms, synthetics, the works. Everything but transportation."

"Well, that's sitting out on the spaceport. That black space yacht on Ramp Three." Sinclair smiled. "Get your gear aboard and make yourselves at home. I'll be ready to blast off in half an hour."

Astro turned to Keene. "Thanks a lot, sir. It was swell of you to set us up this way."

Keene slapped him on the shoulder. "Go on. Have a good time."

Shaking hands all around and saying quick good-bys, the three boys hurried out to stow their gear aboard Sinclair's luxurious space yacht. While Roger and Tom relaxed in the comfortable main cabin, Astro hurried below to inspect the power deck.

Roger laughed as the big cadet disappeared down the hatch. "That guy would rather play with a rocket tube than do anything else in the universe!"

"Yes," said Tom. "He's a real lucky guy."

"How?"

"Ever meet anyone that didn't love that big hick?"

"Nope," said Roger with a sly grin. "And that goes for me too! But don't you ever tell him!"

MAJOR CONNEL HAD BEEN WAITING to see the Solar Alliance Delegate from Venus for three hours. And Major Connel didn't like to wait for anyone or anything. He had read every magazine in the lavish outer office atop the Solar Guard Building in downtown Venusport, drunk ten glasses of water, and was now wearing a path in the rug as he paced back and forth in front of the secretary who watched him shyly.

The buzzer on the desk finally broke the silence and the girl answered quickly as Connel stopped and glared at her expectantly. She listened for a second, then replacing the receiver, turned to the seething Solar Guard officer and smiled sweetly. "Delegate James will see you now, Major."

"Thank you," said Connel gruffly, trying hard not to take his impatience out on the pretty girl. He stepped toward an apparently solid wall that suddenly slid back as he passed a light beam and entered the spacious office of E. Philips James, Venusian Delegate to the Grand Council of the Solar Alliance.

E. Philips James was a small man, with small hands that were moving nervously all the time. His head was a little too large for his narrow body that was clothed in the latest fashion, and his tiny black mustache was carefully trimmed. As Connel stalked into the room, James bounced out of his chair to meet him, smiling warmly.

"Major Connel! How delightful to see you again," he said, extending a perfumed hand.

"You could have seen me a lot sooner," growled Connel. "I've been sitting outside for over three hours!"

James lifted one eyebrow and sat down without making any comment. A true diplomat, E. Philips James never said anything unless it was absolutely necessary. And when he spoke, he never really said very much. He sat back and waited patiently for Connel to cool off and get to the point of his call.

In typical fashion, Connel jumped to it without any idle conversational prologue. "I'm here on a security assignment. I need confidential information."

"Just one moment, Major," said James. He flipped open his desk intercom and called to his secretary outside. "Record this conversation, please."

"Record!" roared Connel. "I just told you this was secret!"

"It will be secret, Major," assured James softly. "The record will go into the confidential files of the Alliance for future reference. A precaution, Major. Standard procedure. Please go on."

Connel hesitated, and then, shrugging his shoulders, continued, "I want to know everything you know about an organization here on Venus known as the Venusian Nationalists."

James's expression changed slightly. "Specific information, Major? Or just random bits of gossip?"

"No rocket wash, Mr. James. Information. Everything you know!"

"I don't know why you've come to me," replied James, visibly annoyed at the directness of the rough spaceman. "I know really very little."

"I'm working under direct orders of Commander Walters," said Connel grimly, "who is also a delegate to the Solar Council. His position as head of the Solar Guard is equal to yours in every respect. This request comes from his office, not out of my personal curiosity."

"Ah, yes, of course, Major," replied James. "Of course."

The delegate rose and walked over to the window, seemingly trying to collect his thoughts. After a moment he turned back. "Major, the organization you speak of is, so far as I know, an innocent group of Venusian farmers and frontier people who meet regularly to exchange information about crops, prices, and the latest farming methods. You see, Major"—James's voice took on a slightly singsong tone, as though he were making a speech—"Venus is a young planet, a vast new world, with Venusport the only large metropolis and cultural center. Out in the wilderness, there are great tracts of cultivated land that supply food to the planets of the Solar Alliance and her satellites. We are becoming the breadbasket of the universe, you might say." James smiled at Connel, who did not return the smile.

"Great distances separate these plantations," continued James. "Life is hard and lonely for the Venusian plantation owner. The Venusian Nationalists are, to my knowledge, no more than a group of landowners who have gotten together and formed a club, a fraternity. It's true they speak the Venusian dialect, these groups have taken names from the old Venusian explorers, but I hardly think it is worthwhile investigating."

"Do they have a headquarters?" Connel asked. "A central meeting place?"

"So far as I know, they don't. But Al Sharkey, the owner of the largest plantation on Venus, is the president of the organization. He's a very amiable fellow. Why don't you talk to him?"

"Al Sharkey, eh?" Connel made a mental note of the name.

"And there's Rex Sinclair, a rather stubborn individualist who wrote to me recently complaining that he was being pressured into joining the organization."

"What kind of pressure?" asked Connel sharply.

James held up his hand. "Don't get me wrong, Major. There was no violence." The delegate suddenly became very businesslike. "I'm afraid that's all the information I can give you, Major." He offered his hand. "So nice to see you again. Please don't hesitate to call on me again for any assistance you feel we can give you."

"Thank you, Mr. James," said Connel gruffly and left the office, a frown creasing his forehead. Being a straightforward person himself, Major Connel could not understand why anyone would hesitate about answering a direct question. He didn't for a moment consider the delegate anything but an intelligent man. It was the rocket wash that went with being a diplomat that annoyed the ramrod spaceman. He shrugged it off. Perhaps he would find out something from Al Sharkey or the other plantation owner, Rex Sinclair.

When he crossed the slidewalk and waited at the curb for a jet cab, Connel suddenly paused and looked around. He felt a strange excitement in the air—a kind of tension. The faces of passing pedestrians seemed strained, intense, their eyes were glowing, as though they all were in on some huge secret. He saw groups of men and women sitting in open sidewalk cafés, leaning over the table to talk to each other, their voices low and guarded. Connel shivered. He didn't like it. Something was happening on Venus and he had to find out what it was before it was too late.

5 "WOW!" EXCLAIMED ROGER.

"Jumping Jupiter!" commented Tom.

"Blast my jets!" roared Astro.

Rex Sinclair smiled as he maneuvered the sleek black

space yacht in a tight circle a thousand feet above the Titan crystal roof of his luxurious home in the heart of the wild Venusian jungle.

"She's built out of Venusian teak," said Sinclair. "Everything but the roof. I wanted to keep the feeling of the jungle around me, so I used the trees right out of the jungle there." He pointed to the sea of dense tropical growth that surrounded the house and cleared land.

The ship nosed up for a thousand yards and then eased back, smoothly braked, to a concrete ramp a thousand yards from the house. The touchdown was as gentle as a falling leaf, and when Sinclair opened the airlock, a tall man in worn but clean fatigues was waiting for them.

"Howdy, Mr. Sinclair," he called, a smile on his lined, weather-beaten face. "Have a good trip?"

"Fine trip, George," replied Sinclair, climbing out of the ship. "I want you to meet some friends of mine. Space Cadets Tom Corbett, Roger Manning, and Astro.

They're going to stay with us during their summer leave while they hunt for tyranno. Boys, this is my foreman, George Hill."

The boys shook hands with the thick-set, muscular man, who smiled broadly. "Glad to meet you, boys. Always wanted to talk to someone from the Academy. Wanted to go there myself but couldn't pass the physical. Bad eyes."

Reaching into the ship, he began lifting out their equipment. "You chaps go on up to the house now," he said. "I'll take care of your gear."

With Sinclair leading the way, the boys slowly walked up a flagstone path toward the house, and they had their first chance to see a Venusian plantation home at close range.

The Sinclair house stood in the middle of a clearing more than five thousand yards square. At the edges, like a solid wall of green vegetation, the Venusian jungle rose more than two hundred feet. It was noon and the heat was stifling. They were twenty-six million miles closer to the sun, and on the equator of the misty planet. While Astro, George, and Sinclair didn't seem to mind the temperature, Tom and Roger were finding it unbearable.

"Can you imagine what it'll be like in the house with that crystal roof!" whispered Roger.

"I'll bet," replied Tom. "But as soon as the sun drops out of the zenith, it should cool off some."

When the group stepped up onto the porch, two house servants met them and took their gear. Then Sinclair and the foreman ushered the cadets inside. They were surprised to feel a distinct drop in temperature.

"Your cooling unit must be pretty large, Mr. Sinclair," commented Tom, looking up at the crystal roof where the sun was clearly visible.

Sinclair smiled. "That's special crystal, mined on Titan at a depth of ten thousand feet. It's tinted, and shuts out the heat and glare of the sun."

George then left to lay out their gear for their first hunt the next morning, and Sinclair took them on a tour of the house. They walked through long corridors looking into all the rooms, eventually winding up in the kitchen, and the three boys marveled at the simplicity yet absolute perfection of the place. Every modern convenience was at hand for the occupant's comfort. When the sun had dropped a little, they all put on sunglasses with glareproof eye shields and walked around the plantation. Sinclair showed them his prize-winning stock and the vast fields of crops. Aside from the main house, there were only four other buildings in the clearing. They visited the smallest, a cowshed.

"Where do your field hands live, Mr. Sinclair?" asked Tom, as they walked through the modern, spotless, milking room.

"I don't have any," replied the planter. "Do most of the work with machinery, and George and the houseboys do what has to be done by hand."

As they left the shed and started back toward the main house they came abreast of a small wooden structure. Thinking they were headed there, Roger started to open the door.

"Close that door!" snapped Sinclair. Roger jerked back. Astro and Tom looked at the planter, startled by the sharpness in his voice.

Sinclair smiled and explained, "We keep some experiments

on different kinds of plants in there at special low temperatures. You might have let in hot air and ruined something."

"I'm sorry, sir," said Roger. "I didn't know."

"Forget it," replied the planter. "Well, let's get back to the house. We're having an early dinner. You boys have to get started at four o'clock in the morning."

"Four o'clock!" exclaimed Roger.

"Why?" asked Tom.

"We have to go deep into the thicket," Astro explained, using the local term for the jungle, "so that at high noon we can make camp and take a break. You can't move out there at noon. It gets so hot you'd fall on your face after fifteen minutes of fighting the creepers."

"Everything stops at noon," added Sinclair. "Even the tyrannosaurus. You have to do your traveling in the cool of the day, early and late. Six hours or so will take you far enough away from the plantation to find tracks, if there are any."

"Tell me, Mr. Sinclair," asked Roger suddenly, "is this the whole plantation?" He spread his hands in a wide arc, taking in the clearing to the edge of the jungle.

Sinclair grinned. "Roger, it'd take a man two weeks to go from one corner of my property to another. This is just where I live. Three years ago I had five hundred square miles under cultivation."

Back in the house, they found George setting the table on the porch and his wife busy in the kitchen. Mrs. Hill was a stout woman, with a pleasant face and a ready smile. With very little ceremony, the cadets, Sinclair, George, and his wife sat down to eat. The food was simple fare, but the sure touch of Mrs. Hill's cooking and the free use of delicate Venusian jungle spices added exotic flavor, new but immensely satisfying to the three hungry boys, a satisfaction they demonstrated by cleaning their plates quickly and coming back for second helpings. Astro, of course, was not happy until he had polished off his fourth round. Mrs. Hill beamed with pleasure at their unspoken compliment to her cooking.

After the meal, Mrs. Hill stacked the dishes and put them into a small carrier concealed in the wall. Pressing a button, near the opening, she explained, "That dingus takes them to the sink, washes them, dries them, and puts everything in its right place. That's the kind of modern living I like!"

As the sun dropped behind the wall of the jungle and the sky darkened, they all relaxed. Sinclair and George smoked contentedly, Mrs. Hill brought out some needle point, and the three cadets rested in comfortable contour chairs. They chatted idly, stopping only to listen to the wild calls of birds and animals out in the jungle as George, or Sinclair, identified them all. George told of his experiences on tyrannosaurus hunts, and Astro described his method of hunting as a boy.

"I was a big kid," he explained. "And since the only way of earning a living was by working, I found I could combine business with pleasure. I used to hitch rides over the belt and parachute in to hunt for baby tyrannos." He grinned and added, "When I think back, I wonder how I ever stayed in one piece."

"Landsakes!" exclaimed Mrs. Hill. "It's a wonder you weren't eaten alive! Those tyrannos are horrible things."

"I was almost a meal once," confessed Astro sheepishly, and at the urging of the others he described the incident that had cured him of hunting alone in the jungles of Venus with only a low-powered shock blaster.

"If I didn't get it at the base of the brain where the nerve centers aren't so well protected with the first shot, I was in trouble," he said. "I took a lot of chances, but was careful not to tangle with a mama or papa tyrannosaurus.

I'd stalk the young ones. I'd wait for him to feed and then let him have it. If I was lucky, I'd get him with one shot, but most of the time I'd just stun him and have to finish him off with a second blast. Then I'd skin him, take the hams and shoulders, and get out of there fast before the wild dogs got wind of the blood. I'd usually hunt pretty close to a settlement where I could get the meat frozen. After that, I'd just have to call a couple of the big restaurants in Venusport and get the best price. I used to make as much as fifty credits on one kill."

"How would you get the meat to Venusport?" asked Roger, who, for all his braggadocio, was awed by his unit mate's calm bravery and skill as a hunter.

"The restaurant that bought it would send a jet boat out for it and I'd ride back with it. After a while the restaurant owners got to know me and would give me regular orders. I was trying to fill a special order on that last hunt."

"What happened?" asked Tom, equally impressed with Astro's life as a boy hunter.

"I had just about finished hunting in a section near a little settlement on the other side of Venus," began the big cadet, "but I thought there might be one more five-hundred-pound baby around, so I dropped in." Astro paused and grinned. "I didn't find a baby, I found his mother! She must have weighed twenty-five or thirty tons. Biggest tyranno I've ever seen. She spotted me the same time I saw her and I didn't even stop to fire. I never could have dented her hide. I started running and she came after me. I made it to a cave and went as far back inside as I could. She stuck her head in after me, and by the craters of Luna, she was only about three feet away, with me backed up against a wall. She tried to get farther in, opened her mouth, and snapped and roared like twenty rocket cruisers going off at once."

Tom gulped and Roger's eyes widened.

"I figured there was only one thing to do," continued Astro. "Use the blaster, even though it couldn't do much damage. I let her have one right in the eye!" Astro shook his head and laughed. "You should have seen her pull her head out of that cave! I couldn't sleep for months after that. I used to dream that she was sticking her head in my window, always getting closer."

"Did the blaster do any damage at all?" asked Sinclair.

"Oh, yes, sir," said Astro. "I was close enough for the heat charge from the muzzle to get her on the side of the head. Nothing fatal, but she's probably still out there in the jungle more ugly than ever with half a face."

The group fell silent, each thinking of how he would have reacted under similar conditions; each silently thankful that it hadn't happened to him. Finally Mrs. Hill rose and said good night, and George excused himself to take a last look at the stock. Remembering their early call for the next morning, the cadets said good night to Sinclair and retired to their comfortable rooms. In bed at last, each boy stretched full length on his bed and in no time was sound asleep.

It was still dark, an hour and a half before the sun would burst over the top of the jungle, when Sinclair went to the cadets' room to rouse them. He found them already up and dressed in their jungle garb. Each boy was wearing skin-tight trousers and jerseys made of double strength space-suit cloth and colored a dark moldy green. A hunter dressed in this manner and standing still could not be seen at twenty paces. The snug fit of the suit was protection against thorns and snags that could find no hold on the hard, smooth-surfaced material.

After a hearty breakfast the three cadets collected their gear, the paralo-ray pistols, the shock rifles, and the small shoulder packs of synthetic food and camping equipment. Each boy also carried a two-foot jungle knife with a compass inlaid in the handle. A helmet of clear plastic with a small mesh-covered opening in the face covered each boy's head. Dressed as they were, they could walk through the worst part of the jungles and not get so much as a scratch.

"Well," commented Sinclair, looking them over, "I guess you boys have everything. I'd hate to be the tyranno that crosses your path!"

The boys grinned. "Thanks for everything, sir," said Tom. "You've been a lot of help."

"Think nothing of it, Tom. Just bring back a pair of tyranno scalps!"

"Where are Mr. and Mrs. Hill?" asked Astro. "We'd like

to say good-by to them."

"They left before you got up," replied Sinclair. "They're taking a few days off for a visit to Venusport."

The boys pulled on their jungle boots. Knee-length and paper-thin, they were nonetheless unpenetrable even if the boys should step on one of the needle-sharp ground thorns.

They waved a last good-by to their host, standing on the steps of the big house, and moved across the clearing to the edge of the jungle wall.

As the cadets approached the thick tangle of vines, the calls and rustling noises from the many crawling things hidden in the forbidding thicket slowly died down. They walked along the edge of the tangle of jungle creepers until they found an opening and stepped through.

After walking only ten feet they were completely surrounded by the jungle and could not even see the clearing they had just left. It was dark, the network of vines, the thick tree trunks and rank growing vegetation shutting out

the sun, leaving the interior of the jungle strangely plunged in gloom. Astro moved ahead, followed by Roger, with Tom bringing up the rear. They followed the path they had entered, as far as it went, and then began cutting their way through the underbrush, stopping only to cut notches in the trees to mark their passage.

Their long-bladed knives slicing through vines and brush easily, Tom, Roger, and Astro hacked their way deeper and deeper into the mysterious and suffocating green world.

6 **"I GUESS THAT'S THE SHARKEY PLACE OVER THERE,"** mumbled Major Connel to himself, banking his jet launch over the green jungles and pointing the speedy little craft's nose toward the clearing in the distance. The Solar Guard officer wrenched the scout around violently in his approach. He was still boiling over the Venusian Delegate's indifference toward his mission.

The launch skimmed the jungle treetops and glided to a perfect stop near the largest of a group of farm buildings. Cutting the motors, Connel sat and waited for someone to appear. He sat there for ten minutes but no one came out to greet him. Finally he climbed out of the launch and stood by the hatch, peering intently at the buildings around him, his eyes squinting against the glare of the fiery sun overhead. The plantation seemed deserted. Reaching back into the launch and pulling out a paralo-ray gun, he strapped its reassuring bulk to his side and stepped toward the building that was obviously the main house. Nothing else moved in the hot noon sun.

As he strode purposefully toward the house, eyes alert for any sign of life, he thought for a moment everyone might be taking a midday nap. Many of the Venusian colonists adapted the age-old custom of the tropics to escape the intense heat of midday. But he dismissed the thought immediately, realizing that his approach in the jet would have awakened the deepest of sleepers.

Entering the house, he stopped in the spacious front hall and called: "Hello! Anybody home? Halloo!"

The only answer was the echo of his own voice, vibrating through the large rooms.

"Funny," muttered the spaceman. "Why is this place deserted?"

He walked slowly through the house, opening doors and looking into all the rooms, searching the whole place thoroughly before returning to the clearing. Going to the nearest of the outbuildings, he opened one of the wide doors and stared into the gloomy interior. With his experienced eye he saw immediately that the building had been used to house a large jet craft. There was the slightly pungent odor of jet fuel, and on the floor the tire marks of a dolly used to roll the craft out to the launching strip. He followed the tracks outside and around to the side of the building where he saw the dolly. It was empty.

Shaking his head grimly, Connel made a quick tour of the remaining buildings. They were all deserted but the last one, which seemed to be built a little more sturdily than the others. Unlike the others, it was locked. He looked for a window and discovered that the walls were solid. There were no openings except the locked door. He hesitated in front of the door, looking down at the ground for a sign of what might have been stored in the building. The surrounding area revealed no tracks. He pulled out a thick-bladed pocketknife and stepped to the lock, then suddenly stopped and grinned.

"Great," he said to himself. "A Solar Guard officer about to break into private property without a warrant. Fine thing to have known back at the Academy!"

He turned abruptly and strode back to the scout. Climbing into the craft, he picked up the audioscriber microphone and recorded a brief message. Removing the threadlike tape from the machine, he returned to the house and left it on the spool of the audioscribe-replay machine near the front door.

A few moments later the eerie silence of the Sharkey plantation was once again shattered by the hissing roar of jets as the launch took off and climbed rapidly over the jungle. Air-borne, Connel glanced briefly at a chart, changed course, and sent the launch hurtling at full speed across the jungle toward the Sinclair plantation.

"HOW FAR DO YOU THINK WE'VE COME?" asked Tom sleepily.

Astro yawned and stretched before answering. "I'd say about fifteen miles, Tom."

"Seems more like a hundred and fifteen," moaned Roger who was sprawled on the ground. "I ache all over. Start at the top of my head and work down, and you won't find one square inch that isn't sore."

Tom grinned. He was tired himself, but the three-day march through the jungle had been three of the most exciting days in his life. Coming from a large city where he had to travel two hours by monorail to get to open green country, the curly-haired cadet found this passage through the wildest jungle in the solar system new and fascinating. He had seen flowers of every color in the spectrum, some as large as himself; giant shrubs with leaves so fine that they looked like spider webs; Venusian teakwood trees fifty to a hundred feet thick at the base with some twisted into strange spirals as their trunks, shaded by another larger tree, sought a clear avenue to the sun. There were bushes that grew thorns three inches long, hard as steel and thin as needles; jungle creepers, vines two and three feet thick, twisting around tree trunks and strangling them.

He saw animals too, all double the size of anything on Earth because of the lighter Venusian gravity; insects the size of rats, rats the size of dogs, and wild dogs the size of ponies. Up in the trees, small anthropoids, cousins to the monkeys of Earth, scampered from limb to limb, screaming at the invaders of their jungle home. Smooth-furred animals that looked like deer, their horns curling overhead, scampered about the cadets like puppies, nuzzling them, nipping at their heels playfully, and barking as though in laughter when Astro roared at them for getting in the way.

But there were dangerous creatures in the jungle too; the beautiful but deadly poisonous brush snakes that lurked unseen in the varicolored foliage, striking out at anything that passed; animals resembling chipmunks with enlarged razor-sharp fangs, whose craving for raw meat was so great that they would attack an animal ten times its size; lizards the size of elephants with scales like armor plate that rooted in swampy ground for their food, but which would attack any intruder, charging with amazing speed, their three horns poised; and, finally, there were the monsters of Venus—giant beasts whose weights were measured in tons, ruled over by the most horrible of them all—the tyrannosaurus.

Fights to death between the jungle creatures were common sights for the boys during their march. They saw a weird soundless fight between a forty-foot snake and a giant vulture with talons nearly two feet across and a beak resembling a mammoth nutcracker. The vulture won, methodically cutting the reptile's body into sections, its beak slicing through the snake as easily as a knife going through butter.

More than once Astro spotted a dangerous creature, and telling Roger and Tom to stand back, he would level his shock rifle and blast it.

So far they had seen nothing of their prey—the tyrannosaurus. Tracks around the steaming swamps were as close as they had come. Once, late in the evening of the second day they caught a fleeting glimpse of a plant-eating brontosaurus lumbering through the brush.

All three of the boys had found it difficult to sleep in the jungle. The first two nights they had taken turns at staying on guard and tending the campfire. Nothing had bothered them, and on the third night out, they decided the fire would be enough to scare off the jungle animals. It was risky, but the continual fight through the jungle underbrush had tired the three boys to the bone and the few hours they stood guard were sorely missed the next day, so they decided to chance it.

Roger was already asleep. Astro had just finished checking his rifle to be ready for instant fire, when Tom threw the last log on the campfire and crawled into his sleeping bag.

"Think it'll be all right, Astro?" asked Tom. "I'm not anxious to wake up inside one of these critter's stomachs."

"Most of them have never seen fire, Tom," Astro said reassuringly. "It scares them. Besides, we're getting close to the big stuff now. You might see a tyranno or a big bronto any time. And if they come along, you'll hear 'em, believe me. They're about as quiet as a squadron of cruisers on battle emergency blasting off from the Academy in the middle of the night!"

"OK," replied Tom. "You're the hunter in this crew." Suddenly he laughed. "You know I really got a bang out of the way Roger jumped back from that waddling ground bird yesterday."

Astro grinned. "Yeah, the one thing in this place that's as ferocious as a kitten and he pulls his ray gun like an ancient cowboy!"

A very tired voice spoke up from the other sleeping bag. "Is that so! Well, when you two brave men came face to face

with that baby lizard on a tree root, you were ready to finish your leave in Atom City!" Roger unzipped the end of the
bag, stuck his blond head out, and gave his unit mates a
sour look. "Sack in, will you? Your rocket wash is keeping
me awake!"

Laughing, Astro and Tom nodded good night to each
other and closed their sleeping bags. The jungle was still,
the only movement being the leaping tongues of flame from
the campfire.

An hour later it began to rain, a light drizzle at first
that increased until it reached the steady pounding of a
tropical downpour. Tom awoke first, opening the flap of his
sleeping bag only to get his face full of slimy water that
spilled in. Spluttering and coughing he sat up and saw that
the campfire was out and the campsite was already six
inches deep in water.

"Roger, Astro!" he called and slapped the nearest sleeping bag. Astro opened the flap a little and peered out sleepily. Instantly he rolled out of the bag and jumped to his feet.

"Wake Roger up!" he snapped. "We've got to get out of
here!"

"What's the matter?" Roger mumbled through the bag,
not opening it. "Why the excitement over a little rain?"

"The fire's out, hotshot," said Astro. "It's as dark as the
inside of a cow's number-four belly. We've got to move!"

"Why?" asked Tom, not understanding the big cadet's
sudden nervous excitement. "What's the matter with staying
right where we are? Why go trooping around in the dark?"

"We can't light a fire anywhere," added Roger, finally
sticking his head out of his sleeping bag.

"We've got to get on high ground!" said Astro, hurriedly
packing the camping equipment. "We're in a hollow here.
The rain really comes down on Venus, and in another hour
this place will be a pond!"

Sensing the urgency in Astro's voice, Roger began
packing up his equipment and in a few moments the three
boys had their gear slung over their shoulders and were
slogging through water already knee-deep.

"I still don't see why we have to go tracking through the
jungle in the middle of the night," grumbled Roger. "We

could climb up a tree and wait out the storm."

"You'd have to wait long after the rain stops," replied Astro. "There is one thing in this place nothing ever gets enough of, and that's water. Animals know it and hang around all the water holes. If a small animal tries to get a drink, he more than likely winds up in something's stomach. When it rains like this, hollows fill up like the one we just left, and everything within running, hopping, and crawling distance heads for it to get a bellyful of water. In another hour our camp will be like something out of a nightmare, with every animal in the jungle coming down for a drink and starting to fight one another."

"Then if we stayed there—" Roger stopped.

"We'd be in the middle of it," said Astro grimly. "We wouldn't last two minutes."

Walking single file, with Astro in the lead, followed by Roger and then Tom, they stumbled through the pitch-black darkness. Astro refused to shine a light, for fear of being attacked by a desperate animal, more eager for water than afraid of the light. They carried their shock blasters cocked and ready to fire. The rain continued, increasing in fury until they were enveloped in a nearly solid wall of water. In a little while the floor of the jungle became one continuous mudhole, with each step taking them ankle-deep into the sucking mud. Their climb was uphill, and the water from above increased, washing down around them in torrents. More than once one of the cadets fell, gasping for breath, into the dirty water, only to be jerked back to more solid footing by the other two. Stumbling, their hands groping wildly in the dark, they pushed forward.

They were reaching higher ground when Astro stopped suddenly. "Listen!" he whispered hoarsely.

The boys stood still, the rain pounding down on their plastic headgear, holding rifles ready and straining their ears for some sound other than the drumming of rain.

"I don't hear anything," said Roger.

"*Shhh!*" hissed Astro.

They waited, and then from a distance they heard the faint crashing of underbrush. Gradually it became more distinct until there was no mistaking its source. A large monster was moving through the jungle near them!

"What is it?" asked Tom, trying to keep his voice calm.

"A big one," said Astro. "A real big one. And I think it's heading this way!"

"By the craters of Luna!" gasped Roger. "What do we do?"

"We either run, or stay here and try to blast it."

"Whatever you say, Astro," said Roger. "You're the boss."

"Same here," said Tom. "Call it."

Astro did not answer right away. He strained his ears, listening to the movements of the advancing monster, trying to ascertain the exact direction the beast was taking. The noise became more violent, the crashing more sharply defined as small trees were crushed to the ground.

"If only I knew exactly what it is!" said Astro desperately. "If it's a tyranno, it walks on its hind legs and has its head way up in the trees, and could pass within ten feet of us and not see us. But if it's a bronto, it has a long snake-like neck that he pokes all around and he wouldn't miss us at a hundred feet!"

"Make up your mind quick, big boy," said Roger. "If that thing gets any closer, I'm opening up with this blaster. He might eat me, but I'll sure make his teeth rattle first!"

The ground began to shake as the approaching monster came nearer. Astro remained still, ears straining for some sound to indicate exactly what was crashing down on them.

Above them, the shrill scream of an anthropoid suddenly pierced the dark night as its tree home was sent crashing to the ground. There was a growing roar and the crashing stopped momentarily.

"Let's get out of here," said Astro tensely. "That's a tyranno, but he's down on all fours now, looking for that monkey! Keep together and make as little noise as you can. No talking. Keep your blasters and emergency lights ready. If he discovers us, you shine the light on his face Roger, and Tom and I will shoot. OK?"

Tom and Roger agreed.

"All right," said Astro, "let's go—and spaceman's luck!"

7 "WHAT CAN I DO FOR YOU, OFFICER?"

Connel heaved his bulk out of the jet launch and looked hard at the man standing in front of him. "You Rex Sinclair?"

Sinclair nodded. "That's right."

Connel offered his hand. "Major Connel, Solar Guard."

"Glad to meet you," replied the planter, gripping the spaceman's hand. "Have something to cool you off."

"Thanks," said Connel. "I can use it. Whew! Must be at least one-twenty in the shade."

Sinclair chuckled. "This way, Major."

They didn't say anything more until Connel was resting comfortably in a deep chair, admiring the crystal roof of Sinclair's house. After a pleasant exchange about crops and problems of farming on Venus, the gruff spaceman squared his back and stared straight at his host. "Mr. James, the Solar Delegate, told me you've resisted pressure to join the Venusian Nationalists."

Sinclair's expression changed slightly. His eyebrows lifting quizzically. "Why—yes, that's true."

"I'd like you to tell me what you know about the organization."

"I see," mused Sinclair. "Is that an order?" he added, chuckling.

"That's a request. I'd like to learn as much about the Nationalists as possible."

"For what purpose?"

Connel paused and then said casually, "A spot check. The Solar Guard likes to keep its eyes open for trouble."

"Trouble?" exclaimed Sinclair. "You're not serious!"

Connel nodded his head. "It's probably nothing but a club. However, I'd like to get some facts on it."

"Have you spoken to anyone else?" asked Sinclair.

"I just came from the Sharkey plantation. It's deserted.

Not a soul around. I'll drop back by there before I return to Venusport." Connel paused and looked squarely at Sinclair. "Well?"

"I don't know much about them, Major," replied the planter. "It always seemed to me nothing more than a group of planters getting together—"

Connel cut him off. "Possibly, but why didn't you join?"

"Well—"

"Aren't all your friends in it?"

"Yes, but I just don't have time. I have a big place, and there's only me and my foreman and housekeeper now. All the field hands left some time ago."

"Where'd they go?"

"Venusport, I guess. Can't get people to farm these days."

"All right, Mr. Sinclair," declared Connel, "let's lay our cards on the table. I know how you must feel talking about your friends, but this is really important. Vitally important to every citizen in the Solar Alliance. Suppose the Nationalists were really a tight organization with a purpose—a purpose of making Venus independent of the Solar Alliance. If they succeeded, if Venus did break away, Mercury might follow, then Mars—the whole system fall apart—break up into independent states. And when that happens, there's trouble—customs barriers, jealousies, individual armies and navies, and then, ultimately, a space war. It's more than just friendship, Sinclair, it's the smallest crack in the solid front of the Solar Alliance, but it's a crack that *can* be opened further if we don't stop it now."

Sinclair was impressed. "Very well, Major, I'll tell you everything I know about them. And you're right, it is hard to talk about your friends. I've grown up here in the Venusian jungle. I helped my father clear this land where the house is built. Most of the men in the Nationalists are friends of mine, but"—he sighed—"you're right, I can't allow this to happen to the Solar Alliance."

"Allow what to happen?" asked Connel.

"Just what you said, about Venus becoming an independent state."

"Tell me all you know," said Connel.

"The group began to form about three years ago. Al

Sharkey came over here one night and said a group of the planters were getting together every so often to exchange information about crops and farming conditions. I went a few times, we all did, on this part of Venus. At first it was fun. We even had picnics and barn dances every three or four weeks. Then one night someone suggested we come dressed in old costumes—the type worn by our forefathers who founded Venus."

Connel nodded.

"Well, one thing led to another," continued Sinclair. "They started talking about the great history of our planet, and complaining about paying taxes to support the Solar Alliance. Instead of opening up new colonies like the one out on Pluto, we should develop our own planet. We stopped dancing, the women stopped coming, and then one night we elected a president. Al Sharkey. The first thing he did was order all members to attend meetings in the dress of our forefathers. He gave the organization a name, the Venusian Nationalists. Right after that, I stopped going. I got tired of listening to speeches about the wonderful planet we live on, and how terrible it was to be governed by men on Earth, millions of miles away."

"Didn't they consider that they had equal representation in the Solar Alliance Chamber?" asked Connel.

"No, Major. There wasn't anything you could say to any of them. If you tried to reason with them, they called you a—a—" Sinclair stopped and turned away.

"What did they call you?" demanded Connel, getting madder by the minute.

"Anyone that disagreed with them was called an Earthling."

"And you disagreed?" asked Connel.

"I quit," said Sinclair stoutly. "And right after that, I started losing livestock. I found them dead in the pens, poisoned. And some of my crops were burned."

"Did you protest to the Solar Guard?"

"Of course, but there wasn't any proof any one of my neighbors had done it. They don't bother me any more, but they don't speak to me either. It's as though I had a horrible disease. There hasn't been a guest in this house in nearly two years. Three space cadets are the first visitors here since I quit the organization."

"Space Cadets?" Connel looked at the planter quizzically.

"Yes, nice young chaps. Corbett, Manning, and a big fellow named Astro. They're out in the jungle now, hunting for tyrannosaurus. I met them through a friend in Venusport and invited them to use my house as a base of operations. Do you know them?"

Connel nodded. "Very well. Finest cadet unit at the Academy. How long have they been in the jungle?"

"About four and a half days now."

"Hope they get themselves a tyranno. But at the same time"—Connel couldn't help chuckling—"if they do, Space Academy will never hear the end of it!"

Suddenly the hot wilting silence around the house was shattered by a thunderous roar. Connel jumped up, followed Sinclair to the window, and stared out over the clearing. They saw what appeared to be a well-organized squadron of jet boats come in for a landing with near military precision. The doors opened quickly and men poured out onto the dusty field. They were dressed alike in coveralls with short quarter-length space boots and round plastic crash helmets. Each man carried a paralo-ray gun strapped to his hips. The uniforms were a brilliant green, with a white band across the chest. The men formed ranks, waited for a command from a man dressed in darker green, and then marched up toward the house.

"By the craters of Luna!" roared Connel. "Who are they?"

"The Nationalists!" cried Sinclair. "They threatened to burn down my house and destroy my farm if I wrote that letter to the delegate. They've come to carry out their threat!"

Connel pulled the paralo-ray gun from his hip and gripped it firmly. "Do you want those men in your house?" he asked Sinclair.

"No—no, of course not!"

"Then you have Solar Guard protection."

"How—?" Sinclair asked. "There are no Solar Guardsmen around here!"

"What in blazes do you think I am, man!" roared Connel as he lunged for the door and stepped out onto the porch. The men were within a hundred feet of the porch when they saw Connel. The Solar Guard officer spread his legs and stuck out his jaw, his paralo-ray gun leveled. "The first one of you tin soldiers that puts a foot on these steps gets frozen stiffer than a snowball on Pluto! Now stand where you are, state your business, and then *blast off!*"

"Halt!" The leader of the column of men held up his hand. Connel saw that the plastic helmets were frosted over, except for a clear band across the eye level. All of the faces were hidden. The leader stepped forward, his hand on his paralo-ray gun. "Greetings, Major Connel."

Connel snorted. "If you'd take off that Halloween mask, I might know who I'm talking to!"

"My name is Hilmarc."

"Hilmarc?"

"Yes. I am the leader of this detachment."

"Leader, huh?" grunted Connel. "Leader of what? A bunch of little tin soldiers?"

"You shall see, Major." Hilmarc's voice was low and threatening.

"I'm going to count to five," announced Connel grimly, lifting his paralo-ray gun, "and if you and your playmates aren't back in your ships, I start blasting."

"That would be unwise," replied Hilmarc. "Your one gun against all of ours."

Connel grinned. "I know. It's going to be a whale of a fight, isn't it?" Then, without pause, he shouted, *"One—two—three—four—five!"*

He opened fire, squeezing the trigger rapidly. The first row of green-clad men were immediately frozen. Dropping to one knee, the spaceman again opened fire, and men in the second row stiffened as they tried to return the fire.

"Fire! Cut him down!" roared Hilmarc frantically.

The men broke ranks and the area in front of Sinclair's house crackled with paralo-ray gunfire. Darting behind a chair, Connel dropped to the floor, his gun growing hot under the continuous discharge of paralyzing energy. In a matter of moments the Solar Guard officer had frozen nearly half of the attacking troop, their bodies scattered in various positions. Suddenly his gun spit fire and began to smoke. The energy charge was exhausted. Connel jumped to his feet and snapped to attention. He knew from experience that if being hit was inevitable, the best way to receive the charge was by standing at attention, taking the strain off the heart. He faced the clearing and a dozen shots of paralyzing energy hit him simultaneously. He became rigid and the short furious battle was over.

One of the green-clad men released Hilmarc from the effects of Connel's ninth shot and he stepped forward to stare straight into Connel's eyes. "I know you can hear me, Major. I want to compliment you on your shooting. But your brave resistance now is as futile as the resistance of the entire Solar Guard in the near future."

Hilmarc smiled arrogantly and stepped back. "Now, if you'll excuse me, I will attend to the business I came here for—to take care of a weakling and an informer!" He turned and shouted to his men. "You have your orders! Get Sinclair and then burn everything in sight."

"ASTRO, TOM," GASPED ROGER. "I—I can't go on."

The blond-haired cadet fell headlong to the ground, almost burying himself in the mud. Tom and Astro turned without a word, and gripping Roger under each arm, helped him to his feet. Behind them, the thunder of the stalking tyrannosaurus came closer, and they forced themselves to greater effort. For two days they had been running before the monster. It was a wild flight through a wild jungle that offered them little protection. And while their fears were centered on the brute behind them, their sleepy, weary eyes sought out other dangers that lay ahead. More than once they stopped to blast a hungry, frightened beast that barred their path, leaving it for the tyrannosaurus and giving themselves a momentary respite in their flight.

Astro led the way, tirelessly slashing at the vines and creepers with his jungle knife, opening the path for Roger and Tom. The Venusian cadet was sure that they were near the clearing around the Sinclair plantation. Since early morning he had seen the trail markers they had left when they started into the jungle. The cadets knew that if they didn't reach the clearing soon they would have to stand and fight the terrible thing that trailed them. During the first wild night, they had stumbled into a sinkhole, and as Tom wallowed helplessly in the clinging, suffocating mud, Astro and Roger stood and fought the giant beast. The shock rifles cracked against the armorlike hide of the monster, momentarily stunning him, but in the darkness and rain, they were unable to get a clear head shot. When Tom finally pulled himself out of the mudhole, they struggled onward through the jungle, with only one shot left in each blaster.

"How much farther, Astro?" asked Tom, his voice weak with fatigue. "I'm starting to fold too."

"Not too far now, Tom," the big cadet assured him. "We should be hitting the clearing soon now." He turned and looked back. "If we could only get a clear shot at that brute's head!"

"Hang on, Roger," said Tom. "Just a little more now."

Roger didn't answer, merely bobbing his head in acknowledgment.

Behind them, the crashing thunderous steps seemed to be getting closer and Astro drove himself harder, slashing at the vines and tangled underbrush, sometimes just bursting through by sheer driving strength. But the heavy-footed creature still stalked them ponderously.

Suddenly Astro stopped and sniffed the air. "Smoke!" he cried. "We're almost there!"

Tom and Roger smiled wanly and they pushed on. A moment later the giant cadet pointed through the underbrush. "There! I see the clearing! And—by the stars—there's a fire! The house is burning!"

Forgetting the danger behind them, the three boys raced toward the clearing. Just before they emerged from the jungle, they stopped and stood openmouthed with astonishment, staring at the scene before them.

"By the craters of Luna!" gasped Astro. "Look!"

The outbuildings of the plantation were burning furiously, sending up thick columns of smoke. The wind blew the dense fumes toward them and they began to cough and gag. Through the smoke they saw a strange array of jet craft in the clearing. Then suddenly their attention was jerked back to another danger. The tyrannosaurus was nearly upon them.

"Run!" roared Astro. He broke for the clearing, followed by Roger and Tom. Once in the open, the boys ran several hundred yards to the nearest jet craft, and safely in the hatch, turned to see the monster come to the edge of the clearing and stop. They saw the brute clearly for the first time.

It stood up on its hind legs, standing almost a hundred feet high. It moved its flat, triangular-shaped head in a slow arc, peering out over the clearing. The smoke billowed around it. It snorted several times in fear and anger. Astro looked at it, wide-eyed, and finally spoke in awed tones. "By the rings of Saturn, it is!"

"Is what?" asked Tom.

"The same tyranno I blasted when I was a kid, the one that trapped me in the cave!"

"Impossible!" snorted Roger. "How can you tell?"

"There on the head, the scars—and that eye. That's the mark of a blaster!"

"Well, I'll be a rocket-headed Earthworm!" said Tom.

The smoke thickened at the moment, and when it cleared again, the great beast was gone. "I guess the smoke chased him away," said Astro. "Smoke!" He whirled around. With the threat of the tyrannosaurus gone, they could face the strange happenings around the clearing.

"Come on," said Tom. He started for the burning buildings in back of the house.

Just at that moment a group of the green-clad men came around the side of the house. Astro grabbed Tom by the arm and pulled him back.

"What's going on here? All these ships, buildings burning, and those men dressed in green. What is it?"

The three boys huddled behind the jet and studied the scene.

"I don't get it," said Tom. "Who are those men? They almost look as if they're soldiers of some kind, but I don't recognize the uniform."

"Maybe it's the fire department," suggested Roger.

"Wait a minute!" roared Tom suddenly. "There on the porch! Major Connel!"

"Omigosh!" said Astro. "It is, but what's the matter with him? Why is he standing there like that?"

"He's been paralo-rayed!" exclaimed Roger. "See how still he is! Whatever these jokers in uniforms are, they're not friendly!" He raised his shock rifle. "This last shot in my blaster should—"

"Wait a minute, Roger," said Tom, "don't go off half-cocked. We can't do much with just three shots. We'd better take over one of these ships. There must be guns aboard."

"Yeah," said Astro. "How about that big one over there?" He pointed to the largest of the assembled crafts.

"OK," said Tom. "Sneak around this side and make a dash for it."

Gripping their rifles, they slipped around the stern of the small ship, and keeping a wary eye on the milling men around the front of the building, they dashed toward the bigger ship.

On the porch of the main house, Major Connel, every muscle in his body paralyzed, saw the three cadets dart across the field and his heart skipped a beat. Immediately before him, two of the green-clad men were holding Sinclair while Hilmarc addressed him arrogantly.

"This is just the beginning, Sinclair. Don't try to cross

us again. Neither you nor anyone else can stop us!" He whirled around and faced Connel. "And as for you and your Solar Guard, Major Connel, you can tell them—"

Hilmarc's tirade was suddenly interrupted by a shrill whistle and the glare of a red flare overhead. There was a chorus of shouts as the men ducked for cover.

A voice, Connel recognized as Tom's, boomed out over the loud-speaker of the large jet ship near the edge of the clearing. "Now hear this! You are covered by an atomic mortar. Drop your guns and raise your hands!"

The men stared at the ship, confused, but Hilmarc issued a curt command. "Return to the ships!"

"But—but he'll blast us," whined one of the men. "He'll kill us all."

"You fool!" roared Hilmarc. "It must be a friend of Connel's or Sinclair's. He won't dare fire an atomic shell near this house, for fear of killing his friends! Now get aboard your ships and blast off!"

From their ship, Tom, Roger, and Astro saw the men scatter across the field, and realizing their bluff had failed, they opened fire with the paralo-ray guns. But their range was too far. In a few moments the clearing around the Sinclair home was alive with the coughing roar of the jets blasting off.

As soon as they were alone, Sinclair snatched up an abandoned ray gun and released the major from the charge. Connel immediately jumped for another gun. But then, as the jets started to take off, he saw that it would be useless to pursue the invaders. Thankful that the cadets had arrived in time, he trotted across the clearing to meet them as they climbed wearily from the remaining jet ship.

"By the craters of Luna," he roared good-naturedly, "you three space-brained idiots had me scared! I thought you would really let go with that mortar!"

Tom and Roger grinned, relieved to find the spaceman unhurt, while Astro looked off at the disappearing fleet of ships.

"What's happened, sir?" asked Tom. "What's it all about?"

"Haven't time to explain now," said Connel. "I just want you three to know you got back here in time to save the rest of this man's property." He turned toward Sinclair, who was just approaching. "Did you recognize any of them?" he asked the planter.

Sinclair shook his head. "I thought I did—by their voices, I mean. But I couldn't see anyone through that frosted headgear they were wearing."

"Well, they left a ship. We'll find out who that belongs to," said Connel. "All right, Corbett, Manning, Astro. Stand by to blast off!"

"Blast off?" exclaimed Roger. "But we're on leave, sir!"

"Not any more, you're not!" snapped Connel. "You're recalled as of now! Get this ship ready to blast off for Venusport in five minutes!"

8 **"ARE YOU SURE THEY WENT SOUTH, ASTRO?"**

Major Connel was examining a map of the Southern Hemisphere of Venus. The three cadets were grouped around him in the small control room of the jet ship.

"I think so, sir," replied Astro. "I watched them circle and then climb. There would be no reason to climb unless they were going over the mountains."

"What do you think, Tom?" asked Connel.

"I don't know, sir. The map doesn't show anything but jungle for about a thousand square miles. Unless there's a secret base somewhere between here and there"—he placed his fingers on the map where the Sharkey and Sinclair plantations were marked—"I don't see where they could have gone."

"Well, that must be the answer, then," sighed the gruff spaceman. "Our alert to the patrol ships in this area narrows it down. Nothing was spotted in the air. And they couldn't have blasted off into space. All their ships were low-flying stuff."

Blasting off from the Sinclair plantation immediately,

the three cadets and the major had hoped to find the operations base of the green-clad invaders, but the ships had disappeared. The ship they had captured proved to be a freighter with no name and all identifying marks removed. They had asked the Solar Guard ship registry in Venusport to check on the vessel's title but so far had received no answer.

Now blasting back to Venusport at full speed, Connel told the boys the real nature of his mission to Venus. The boys were shocked, unable to believe that anyone, or any group of persons, would dare to buck the authority of the Solar Guard. Yet they had seen with their own eyes a demonstration of the strength of the Nationalists. Roger had sent a top-secret teleceiver message to Commander Walters at Space Academy, requesting an immediate conference with Connel, and had received confirmation within a half-hour.

"I think Captain Strong will be along too," said Roger to Tom after Connel had retired to a compartment with a recorder to transcribe a report of the affair at Sinclair's. "The message said we were to prepare a full report for consideration by Commander Walters, Professor Sykes, and Captain Strong."

"Boy," said the curly-haired cadet, "this thing is too big for me to swallow. Imagine a bunch of dopes dressing up in uniforms and burning a guy's buildings because he wrote a letter to his delegate!"

"I'd hate to be a member of that organization when Commander Walters gets through with them," said Roger in a slow drawl. "And particularly the guy that ordered Connel blasted with that ray gun. Ten shots at once! Wow! That guy must have nerves made of steel!"

Within an hour the jet freighter was circling Venusport and was given priority clearance for an immediate landing. Immediately upon landing, the ship swarmed with Solar Guardsmen, grim-faced men assigned to guard it, while technicians checked the ship for identification.

The three boys were still wearing the jungle garb when they presented themselves to Major Connel with the request for a little sleep.

"Take an aspirin!" roared Connel. "We've got important work to do!"

"But, sir," said Roger, his eyes half-closed, "we're dead on our feet! We've been out in the jungle for three days and—"

"Manning," interrupted the spaceman, "everything you saw during that business back at Sinclair's might be valuable. I'm sorry, but I'll have to insist that you talk to the Solar Guard security officers first. As tired as you are, you might forget something after a heavy sleep."

There was little else the boys could do but follow the burly officer out of the ship to a well-guarded jet cab which took them through the streets of Venusport to the Solar Guard headquarters.

They rode the elevator to the conference room in silence, each boy feeling at any moment that he would collapse from exhaustion. In the long corridor they passed tough-looking enlisted guardsmen who were heavily armed, and before being allowed into the conference room, they were scrutinized by a brawny officer. Finally inside, they were allowed to sit down in soft chairs and were given hot cups of tea to drink while precise, careful interrogators took down the story of their first meeting with the Venusian Nationalists. They were forced to repeat details many times, in the hope that something new might be added.

Groggy after nearly two hours of this, the boys felt sure that the time had come for them to be allowed to get some sleep, but after the last question from the interrogators, they were ushered into the presence of Commander Walters, Major Connel, Professor Sykes, Captain Strong, and several recording secretaries. Before the conference began, Delegate E. Philips James arrived with his personal secretary. He offered his excuses for being late and took his place at the long table. Tom shot a glance at the secretary. The man looked vaguely familiar to him. The cadet tried to place him, but he was so tired that he could not think.

"Major Connel," began Commander Walters abruptly, "what do you consider the best possible move for the Solar Guard to make? Under the present circumstances, do you think we should undertake a full-scale investigation? We talked to Al Sharkey, and while he admits being head of an organization known as the Venusian Nationalists, he denies any knowledge of any attack on Sinclair such as you describe. And he claims to have been in Venusport when the incident happened."

Connel thought a moment. "I don't know about Sharkey, but I don't think a public investigation should be made yet. I think it would arouse a lot of speculation and achieve no results."

"Then you think we should move against them merely on the basis of this encounter at the Sinclair plantation," asked E. Philips James in his smoothest manner.

Connel shook his head. "I think our best bet is to locate their base. If we can nail them with solid evidence, we'll have a good case to present before the Grand Council of the Solar Alliance."

"I agree with you, Major." James smiled. Behind him, his secretary was busy transcribing the conversational exchange on his audioscriber.

"What would you require to locate the base?" asked Walters.

"I haven't worked out the details yet," said Connel, "but a small expedition into the jungle would be better than sending a regiment of guardsmen, or a fleet of ships."

"Do you have any idea where the base might be?" Sykes suddenly spoke up. "Most of those men were supposed to be planters who know the jungle well. Isn't it possible that they might have their base well hidden and a small party, such as you suggest, could cover too little ground?"

Connel turned to Astro. "Astro, do you know that section of the belt?"

"Yes, sir," replied Astro. "I hunted all over that area when I was a boy." The big cadet went on to explain how he had become so familiar with the jungle, and described briefly their experience with the tyrannosaurus. All of the men at the table were impressed by his knowledge of jungle lore.

"I gather you plan to take these cadets on your expedition, Major," commented James.

"Yes, I do. They work well together and have already been in the jungle," answered Connel.

"What do you three boys think of the idea?" asked Walters. "I don't have to remind you that you'll be up against two kinds of danger: the jungle itself, and the Nationalists."

"We understand, sir," replied Tom, without even waiting for his unit mates' quick nods.

"There's another factor," Captain Strong broke in. "You'll be giving up your leave. There won't be any extra time off. Should this mission be completed before the next term at the Academy begins, fine. But if not, you'll have to return to work immediately."

"We understand that too, sir," said Tom. "We're willing to do anything we can. And if I might offer a personal opinion"—he glanced at Astro and Roger—"I think the *Polaris* unit appreciates the seriousness of the situation and we agree with the major. A small party, especially ours, since we're already established as hunters, would be less suspect than a larger one."

"I think we all agree that the *Polaris* unit is qualified for the mission, Corbett," said Walters, who saw through Tom's eagerness to be assigned to go with the major.

The meeting broke up soon afterward. Connel remained with Strong and Walters to work out the details of the mission and to draft a top-secret report to the Grand Council of the Solar Alliance.

The three weary cadets were quartered in the finest hotel in Venusport and had just stumbled into bed when the room televiewer signal buzzed. Tom shuffled over to the screen near the table where the remains of a huge supper gave mute evidence of their hunger. Switching on the machine, he saw Strong's face come into focus.

"I hope you boys aren't too comfortable," announced Strong. "I'm afraid the sleep you're so hungry for will have to wait. This is an emergency!"

"Oh, no!" groaned Roger. "I can't understand why emergencies come up every time I try to pound the pillow!"

Astro fell back onto his bed with the look of a martyred saint and groaned.

"What is it, sir?" asked Tom, who was as tired as the others. Nonetheless he felt the urgency in Strong's voice.

"You blast off in half an hour," said the Solar Guard captain. "The *Polaris* has been refitted and you're to check

THE REVOLT ON VENUS

her over before returning to Sinclair's. Everything has been prepared for you. Get dressed and you'll find a jet cab waiting for you in front of the hotel. I had hoped to see you again before you left, but I've been ordered back to the Academy with Commander Walters. We've got to report to the Solar Council, personally."

"OK, sir," said Tom, then smiled and added, "We're sorry your fishing was interrupted."

"I wasn't catching anything, anyway." Strong laughed. "I've got to go. See you back at the Academy. Spaceman's luck!"

"Same to you, sir," replied Tom. The screen blurred and the image faded as the connection was broken. Tom turned to face his sleepy-eyed unit mates. "Well, I guess we'd better take another aspirin. It looks like a hard night!"

Hastily donning fresh jungle gear supplied the night before in anticipation of the mission, the three cadets trouped wearily out of their rooms and rode down to the lobby in the vacuum elevator. They walked across the deserted lobby as though in a trance and outside to the quiet street. A jet cab stood at the curb, the driver watching them. He whistled sharply and waved at them. "Hey, cadets! Over here!"

Still in a fog, the three cadets climbed into the back seat, flopping into the soft cushions with audible groans as the cab shot away from the hotel and sped into the main highway which led to the spaceport.

The traffic was light and the cab zoomed along at a smooth, fast clip, lulling the boys into a fitful doze. But they were rudely awakened when the car spun into a small country lane and the driver slammed on the brakes. He whirled around and grinned at them over a paralo-ray pistol. "Sorry, boys, the ride ends here. Now climb out and start stripping."

The three sleepy cadets came alive instantly. Without a word they moved in three different directions simultaneously. Tom dived for one door, Astro the other, while Roger flopped to the floor. The driver fired, missing all of them, and before he could fire again he was jerked out of his seat and held in a viselike grip by Astro. Tom quickly wrenched the paralo-ray gun from his hand.

"All right, you little space crawler," growled Astro, "start talking!"

"Take it easy, Astro," said Tom. "How do you expect him to talk when you've got him around the Adam's apple?"

"Yeah, you big ape," said Roger in a slow drawl. "Find out what he has to say before you twist his head off!"

Astro released the man, pushing him against the cab door and pinning him there.

"Now let's have it," he growled. "What's this all about?"

"I didn't mean any harm," whined the cab driver. "A guy calls me and says for me to meet three Space Cadets."

"What guy?" snapped Tom.

"A guy I once knew when I was working the fields in the jungle belt. I worked on a plantation as a digger."

"What's his name?" asked Roger.

"I don't know his name. He's just a guy. He calls me and says it's worth a hundred credits to pick up three Space Cadets from the hotel and hold 'em for an hour. I figured the best way to hold you would be to make you take your clothes off."

"What did he look like?" asked Roger.

"A little guy, with a bald head and a limp. That's all I know—honest."

"A limp, eh?" asked Tom. "A little fellow?"

"How little?" asked Astro, getting the drift of Tom's question.

"Real little. About five feet maybe, not much more'n that!"

The three boys looked at each other and nodded.

"The guy we bought our jungle gear from in the pawn-shop!" exclaimed Astro.

"Yeah," said Tom. "It sure sounds like him. But why would he want to stop us? And more important, who told him that Captain Strong was sending a cab for us?"

They turned back to the cab driver for further explanation, but the man was now actually crying with fright.

"We won't get anything more out of this little creep," said Astro. "Let's just turn him over to the Solar Guard at the spaceport. They'll know how to handle him."

"Right," Tom agreed. "We've lost enough time as it is."

"No, no—please!" moaned the cabman. "Lemme go! Take the cab. Drive it to the spaceport and just leave it, but please don't turn me over to the Solar Guard. If I'm seen with them, I'll be—" Suddenly the man darted to one side, eluded Astro's lunge, and scampered away. In a moment he was swallowed up in the darkness.

"Boy," breathed Astro, "he was sure scared of something!"

"Yes," said Tom. "And I'm beginning to get a little scared myself!"

The cadets climbed into the cab and roared off toward the spaceport, each boy with the feeling that he was sitting on a smoldering volcano that was suddenly starting to erupt around him.

9 "ROCKET CRUISER *POLARIS* TO SOLAR GUARD VENUSPORT! REQUEST EMERGENCY RELAY CIRCUIT to Commander Walters en route Earth!"

On the radar bridge of the *Polaris*, Roger Manning spoke quickly into the teleceiver microphone. Just a few minutes before the giant spaceship had blasted off from Venusport, heading for the Sinclair plantation, Major Connel had ordered Roger to get in touch with Walters to report the latest security leak. On the control deck the major paced back and forth restlessly as Tom guided the *Polaris* on its short flight.

"I'll find the spy in the Solar Guard if I have to tear Venusport apart piece by piece!" fumed Connel.

"What about that jet freighter we took away from the Nationalists, sir?" asked Tom. "Did you ever find out where it came from?"

Connel nodded. "It was an old bucket on the Southern Colonial run. She was reported lost last year. Somehow those jokers got hold of her and armed her to the teeth."

"You think maybe the crew could have mutinied, sir?"

"It's highly possible, Corbett," answered Connel, and glanced around. "If they have any other ships of that size, the *Polaris* will be able to handle them."

"Yes, sir." Tom smiled. "The repair crew did a good job on her." The cadet paused. "Do you suppose one of the Nationalists planted that bomb on her fin?"

"No doubt of it," replied Connel. "And it seems to tie in with a rather strange thing that happened in the Venusian Delegate's office the day before it happened."

"What was that, sir?" asked Tom.

"Three priority orders for seats aboard a Venusport— Atom City express were stolen. Before a check could be made, the ship had made its run and the people using the priorities were gone. They must have been the ones that bumped you off your seats."

"How do you think that ties in with the bomb on the *Polaris*, sir?"

"We're trying to figure that out now," said Connel. "If only we knew what they looked like it would help. The girl at the ticket office doesn't remember them and neither does the ship's stewardess."

"But we saw them, sir!" exclaimed Tom.

"You what!" roared Connel.

"Yes, sir. We were standing there at the ticket counter when they called for their tickets."

"Do you think you'd recognize them again?"

"I'll say!" asserted Tom. "And I'm sure Astro and Roger would, too. We were so mad, we could have blasted them on the spot."

Connel turned to the intercom and shouted, "Manning, haven't you got that circuit through yet?"

"Working on it, sir." Roger's voice was smooth and unruffled over the intercom. "I'm in contact with the commander's ship now. They're calling him to the radar bridge now."

Tom suddenly jumped out of his seat as though stung. "Say! I saw one of the fellows again too!"

Connel whirled quickly to face the young cadet. "Where?" he demanded. "Where did you see him?"

"I—I'm trying to remember." Tom began pacing the deck, snapping his fingers impatiently. "It was sometime during the past few days—I know it was!"

"In Venusport?" demanded Connel, following Tom around the deck.

"Yes, sir—"

"Before or after your trip into the jungle?"

"Uhh—before, I think," Tom replied hesitantly. "No. No. It was after we came back."

"Well, out with it, Corbett!" exploded the major. "When? Where? You didn't do that much visiting! You were too tired to move!"

"That's just it, sir," said Tom, shaking his head. "I was so tired everything was a blur. Faces are all mixed up. I—I—" The boy stopped and put his hands to his head as though trying to squeeze the one vital face out of his hazy memory.

Connel kept after him like a hungry, stalking animal. "Where, Corbett? When?" he shouted. "You've got to remember. This is important! Think, blast you!"

"I'm trying, sir," replied the cadet. "But it just won't come to me."

The buzz of the intercom suddenly sounded and Connel reluctantly left Tom to answer it. Roger's voice crackled over the speaker. "I have Commander Walters now, sir. Feeding him down to the control-deck teleceiver."

"Oh, all right," replied Connel and turned to Tom. "Come on, Corbett. I want you to report to the commander personally."

"Yes, sir," replied Tom, walking slowly to the teleceiver. "I'm sorry I can't remember where I saw that man."

"Forget it," Connel said gruffly. "It'll come to you again

sometime." He paused and then added as gently as he could, "Sorry I blasted you like that."

When Commander Walters' face appeared on the teleceiver screen, Connel reported the incident of the cab driver and the news that Tom, Roger, and Astro had seen the three men who had taken the priorities on the *Venus Lark*.

"Just a minute," said Walters. "I'll have a recorder take down the descriptions."

Connel motioned to Tom, who stepped before the screen. When he saw Walters nod, he gave a complete description of the three men he had seen in the Atom City spaceport.

"Let's see, now," said Walters, after Tom had concluded his report. "The man who asked for the tickets was young, about twenty-two, dressed in Venusian clothing, dark, six feet tall, weighed about one hundred and fifty pounds. Right?"

"Yes, sir," replied Tom.

Connel suddenly stepped before the screen to interject, "And Corbett saw him in Venusport again sometime during the last two days."

"Really? Where?"

Connel glanced at Tom and then replied hurriedly, "Well, he can't be sure, sir. We rushed him around pretty fast and he saw a lot of people. But at least we know he's in Venusport somewhere."

"Yes," nodded Walters. "That's something to work on, at least. And you have nothing more to add to the descriptions of the other two, Corbett?"

"Not anything particular, sir," said Tom. "They were dressed in Venusian-type clothes also, but we didn't get a close look at them."

"Very well," said Walters. "Proceed with your mission, Major. I'll have an alert sent out for the cab driver, and I'll have the owner of the pawnshop picked up. There must be someone on the Solar Delegate's staff who stole those priorities. We'll start searching there first, and if we come up with anyone who can't explain his absence from Venusport at the time the priorities were used, and fits Corbett's description, we'll contact you. End transmission!"

"End transmission!" repeated Connel. The screen blanked

out and Roger's voice came over the intercom immediately. "We'll be over Sinclair's in three minutes," he called. "Stand by."

Tom turned to the controls and in exactly two minutes and fifty seconds the clearing surrounding Sinclair's home and the burned outbuildings came into view. Working effortlessly, with almost casual teamwork, the three cadets brought the giant spaceship to rest in the middle of the clearing. As the power was cut, the cadets saw George and Mrs. Hill jumping into a jet car and speeding out to greet them.

After Tom introduced Connel to the couple, the major questioned them closely about their absence during the attack by the shock troops.

"Mr. Sinclair often gives us time off for a trip into Venusport," explained Hill. "It gets pretty lonely out here."

"Is Mr. Sinclair in now?" asked Connel.

"No, he isn't," replied the plantation foreman. "He's on his weekly trip around the outer fields. I don't expect him back for another day or two."

"For goodness sakes," exclaimed Mrs. Hill, "you can ask your questions just as easily and a darn sight more comfortably in the house! Come on. Let's get out of the sun."

The small group climbed into the jet car and roared off across the clearing toward the house. The lone building left standing by the Nationalists looked strange amid the charred ruins of the other buildings. In the house, the three cadets busied themselves with home-baked apple pie which the housekeeper had brought out, while Connel was telling George of the attack on the plantation.

"I've known about them all along, of course," said the foreman. "But I never paid any attention to them. I just quit, like Mr. Sinclair, when they started all that tomfoolery about wearing uniforms and stuff."

"Well," said Connel, accepting a wedge of pie at Mrs. Hill's insistence, "now they've made the wrong move. Burning Sinclair's property and attacking an officer of the Solar Guard is going too far."

"What are you going to do about it?" asked George.

"I'm not at liberty to say, Mr. Hill," replied Connel. "But I can tell you this. When any person, or group of persons, tries to dictate to the Alliance, the Solar Guard steps in and puts a stop to it!"

Suddenly the silence of the jungle clearing was shattered by the roar of a single jet craft coming in for a landing. Without looking out the window, George smiled and said, "There's Mr. Sinclair now! I know the sound of his jets."

The group crowded out onto the front porch while George took the jet car and drove off to pick up his employer. A few moments later Sinclair was seated before Connel, wiping his sweating brow and accepting a cool drink from Mrs. Hill.

"I was on my way to the north boundary when I saw your ship landing," explained Sinclair. "At first I thought it might be those devils coming back, but then I saw the Solar Guard insigne on the ship and figured it might be you." He looked at Connel closely. "Anything new, Major?"

"Not yet," replied Connel. "But you can rest assured that you won't be bothered by them again."

Sinclair paused, eying the major speculatively. "You know, as soon as you left, I went over to talk to Al Sharkey. I was plenty mad and really blasted him, but he swears that he was in Venusport at the time and doesn't know a thing about the raid."

Connel nodded. "That's true. We checked on him. But while he might not have been in on the raid itself, there's nothing that says he didn't order it done!"

"I doubt it," said Sinclair, with a queer apologetic note in his voice. "I'm inclined to believe that it was nothing more than a bunch of the younger, more hotheaded kids in the organization. As a matter of fact, Sharkey told me he was quitting as president. Seems you fellows in Venusport scared him plenty. Not only that, but I heard him calling up the other planters telling them what happened and every one of them is chipping in to rebuild my plantation."

Connel looked at the planter steely-eyed. "So you think it was done by a bunch of kids, huh?"

Sinclair nodded. "Wouldn't be surprised if they're not scared too!"

"Well, you are entitled to your opinion, Mr. Sinclair. And if the other planters are going to rebuild your buildings, that's fine and charitable of them." Suddenly Connel's voice became harsh. "That does not, however, erase the fact that a group of uniformed men, armed with paralo-ray guns and with ships equipped with blasters, attacked you! Atomic blasters, Mr. Sinclair, are not bought at the local credit exchange. They are made exclusively for the Solar Guard! That bunch of hotheaded kids, as you call them, are capable of attacking any community—even ships of the Solar Guard itself! That is a threat to the peace of the solar system and must be stopped!"

Sinclair nodded quickly. "Oh, I agree, Major, I agree. I'm just saying that—"

Connel stopped him. "I understand, Mr. Sinclair. You're a peaceful man and want to keep your life peaceful. But my job is to ensure that peace. As long as a group of militant toughs like we had here are on the loose, you won't have peace. You'll have pieces!"

Tom, Roger, and Astro, sitting quietly and listening, felt like standing up and cheering as the major finished.

"I know you can't tell me what you're going to do, Major Connel," said the planter, "but I hope that you'll allow me to help in any way I can."

Connel hesitated before answering. "Thank you, Mr. Sinclair. But I'm not here officially now." And then he added, "Nor in regard to the Nationalists."

Sinclair's eyes lit up slightly. "Oh?"

"No. As you know, the cadets had quite a time with a tyrannosaurus. They wounded it and it might still be dangerous. That is, more dangerous than normally. I've got orders to track him down and finish him off."

"But I thought you said you were going to put a stop to

this business with the Nationalists," said the planter.

"I said the Solar Guard would, Sinclair."

"Oh, yes," mumbled Sinclair, "the Solar Guard. Of course."

Connel got up abruptly. "I would appreciate it if you would look after our ship, though," he said. "I don't think we'll be longer than a week. Shouldn't be hard to track a tyrannosaurus, especially if it's wounded."

"I suppose you have all the equipment you need," said Sinclair.

"Yes, thank you," replied Connel. Then, thanking Mrs. Hill for the refreshments, the burly spaceman and the three cadets said good-by and left the house.

An hour later, ready to strike off into the jungle, the Solar Guard officer took four of the latest model shock rifles out of the arms locker of the *Polaris* and gave one to each boy with extra ammunition. "Never go after a giant with a popgun," he said. "It's a wonder you didn't kill yourselves with those old blasters you used, let alone kill a tyranno."

The three cadets examined the rifles closely and with enthusiasm.

"These are the latest Solar Guard issue," said Connel.

"When you pull that trigger, you release a force three times greater than anything put into a rifle before."

Then, checking the *Polaris* and cutting all power, Connel removed the master switch and hid it. "That's so no one will get any bright ideas while we're gone," he explained as the boys watched curiously.

"You think someone might try to steal her, sir?" asked Tom.

"You never can tell, Corbett," answered Connel noncommittally.

Once again the three boys moved across the clearing toward the jungle wall. Astro took the lead as before, followed by Roger and Tom, and Connel brought up the rear. They moved directly to the spot where they had last seen the tyrannosaurus, found the trampled underbrush and massive tracks, and moved purposefully into the dank, suffocating green world.

The trail was plain to see. Where the boys once had to hack their way through the thick underbrush, the monster had created a path for them. The three cadets felt better about being back in the jungle with more reliable equipment and joked about what they would do to the tyrannosaurus when they saw it again.

"I thought you were supposed to be the home-grown Venusian hick that could manage in the jungle like that fairy-tale character, Tarzan," Roger teased Astro.

"Listen, you sleepwalking space Romeo," growled Astro, "I know more about this jungle than you could learn in ten years. And I'm not foolish enough to battle with a tyranno with the odds on his side. I ran for a good reason!"

"Boy, did you run!" taunted Roger. "You were as fast as the *Polaris* on emergency thrust!"

"Knock off that rocket wash!" roared Connel. "The Nationalists might have security patrols in this area.

They could hear you talking and blast you before you could bat an eyelash! Now keep quiet and stay alert!"

The three cadets quieted down after that, walking carefully, stepping around dead brush that might betray their presence. After working their way along the tyrannosaurus's trail for several hours, Connel called a halt, and after a quick look at his compass, motioned for them to cut away from the monster's tracks.

"We'll start working around in a circle," he said. "One day east, one south, west, and north. Then we'll move in closer to the heart of the circle, and repeat the same procedure. That should cover a lot of ground in eight days. If anything's moving around out here, besides what should be here, we'll find it. From now on, we'll have a scout. Astro, you know the jungle, you take the point, about five hundred yards ahead. If you see anything, signs of a patrol or any danger from the jungle, fall back and report. Don't try to do anything yourself. Four guns in a good position are better than one popping off by itself."

"Aye, aye, sir," said Astro. With a quick nod to Tom and Roger, he moved off through the jungle. In ten feet he was invisible. In thirty seconds his footsteps were lost in the thousands of jungle sounds around them.

"I'll take the lead now," said Connel. "Corbett, you bring up the rear. All right, move out!"

From above, in the leafy roof covering the jungle; from the side, in the thick tangle of vines; and from below, in the thorny underbrush, the eyes of living things, jungle things, followed the movements of the three spacemen, perhaps wondering if these new beasts were a threat to their lives.

10 "HAL-LOO-OOO!" ASTRO'S VOICE BOOMED OUT over the tops of the trees, where the birds fluttered in sudden fright. It echoed through the darkness around him, where smaller creatures crawled and slithered into the protection of their holes. The voice of the big cadet was loud, but it was not loud enough for his mates to hear.

Astro was lost.

He couldn't understand how it had happened. Over and over during the past six hours he had retraced his steps mentally, trying to visualize the trail, trying to locate the telltale marks he had made with his jungle knife, and so find Major Connel, Tom, and Roger. It was dark now and the big cadet had to face the dangerous jungle alone. He laughed ironically. Connel had given him the point because he knew the jungle! And now he was lost.

Astro was a little frightened too. It was his frank realization of trouble that made him afraid. He knew what was in the jungle, and though he had been there alone before, he had never been in it as deeply as this, nor had he ever been lost in the nightmarish place after sundown.

While he was desperately anxious to find his unit mates, he had not fired his rifle. The threat of exposing his position to a possible Nationalist patrol prevented him from signaling with the blaster or even from building a fire. During the last hours of the day, when the suspicion that he was lost became a concrete fact, the big cadet had been reluctant even to yell. Now, with pitch-black night closing around him, he dared to call, hoping it would be heard and recognized by his friends, or if not, considered the howl of a jungle beast by an enemy patrol, should one be near.

He stood with his back against the rough bark of a teakwood tree to protect his rear and to face out toward the pitch-black night. More than once the big cadet felt the sudden ripple of a crawling thing moving around him, across his toes or down the tree trunk. There was a sudden thrashing in the underbrush nearby and he brought the shock rifle up quickly, ears tuned for the growl, or scream, or hiss of an attacking beast.

The luminous dial of his watch showed it to be three thirty in the morning, two and a half hours to go before the sun would drive the fearful darkness away. He had been calling every five minutes. And every time he shouted, the movements in the darkness around him increased.

"Hal-loo-ooo!"

He waited, turning his head from one side to the other, intent on the sounds that came from a distance; the answering call of the waddling ground bird that had confused him at first until he recognized it; the shrill scream of the tiny swamp hog; the distant chattering of the monkeylike creatures in the treetops. But there was no sound from a human throat.

Astro called again and again. The seconds dragged by into minutes, the minutes into an hour, and then two hours, and finally, as every muscle in his body ached from standing backed up to the tree all night and holding his rifle on alert, the gray murky dawn broke over the jungle and he began to see the green of the jungle around him. When the sun at last broke over the Venusian horizon, the night's frost on the leaves and bushes danced and glittered like jewels.

He washed his face in a near-by pool, careful not to drink any of the water. He opened a can of synthetic food, and after eating his fill, cleared away the brush down to the naked black soil and banking it high on all sides he stretched full length on the ground. He dared not sleep. Hungry animals were moving about freely now. A paralo-ray gun and the rifle, both cocked and ready to fire, were held in his hands. He relaxed as completely as he could, idly watching the mother of a brood of the anthropoids scamper through the branches of the trees overhead, bringing her squalling young their breakfast. An hour later, refreshed, he started through the jungle again, eyes open for signs of recent activity, human activity, for the big cadet wanted to return to his comrades.

Stopping occasionally to climb a tree, Astro searched the sky above the treetops for smoke that would mark a campsite. He felt sure that if there was any, he would find Roger, Tom, and Connel, since a Nationalist patrol wouldn't advertise its presence in the jungle. But there were no smoke signs. The top of the jungle stretched green and still as far as he could see, steaming under the burning rays of the sun.

Astro knew that it would be impossible to spend another night like the first in the jungle, so after searching through the forest until three in the afternoon, he stopped, opened another can of synthetic food, and ate. He was used to being alone now. The first wave of fear had left him and he was beginning to remember things he knew as a young boy; jungle signs that warned him of dangers, the quick identification of the animal cries, and the knowledge of the habits of the jungle creatures.

After eating, he took his jungle knife and hacked at a long, tough vine, yanking it down from its lofty tangle. He started weaving it into a tight oblong basket and two hours later, just before the sun dropped into the jungle for the night, he was finished. He had a seven-foot bag woven tightly and pulled together with a small opening at one end. Just before the sky darkened, the big cadet crawled into this makeshift sleeping bag, pulled the opening closed with a tight draw cord, and in thirty seconds was asleep. Nothing would be able to bite through the tough vine matting, and the chances of a larger beast accidentally stepping on him were small. Nevertheless, Astro had pulled the bag close to a huge tree and placed it deep between the swollen roots.

He awoke with a start. The ground was shaking violently. He was sweating profusely and judged that it must be late in the morning with the sun beating directly on him. Carefully he opened the end of the makeshift sleeping bag and peered out. He gasped and reached for his shock rifle, bringing it up into firing position. The sight that confronted him was at once horrifying and fascinating. A

hundred yards away, a giant snake, easily a hundred feet long and five feet thick, was wrapped around a raging tyrannosaurus. The monsters were in a fight to death. Astro shuddered and pulled back into the bag, keeping the blaster aimed at the two struggling beasts.

The big cadet deduced that the snake must have been surprised in its feeding by the tyrannosaurus, and was trying to defend itself. There wasn't a living thing in the jungle that would deliberately attack a tyrannosaurus.

Only man, with his intelligence and deadly weapons, could win over the brute force and cunning of the jungle giant. And even that had failed with this monster. Astro quickly saw it was the same beast that had chased the three cadets out of the jungle!

With three coils wrapped around the tyrannosaurus's body, the snake was trying to wrap a fourth around its neck and strangle it, but the monster was too wily. Rearing back, it suddenly fell to the ground, its weight crushing the three coils around its middle. The snake jerked spasmodically, stunned, as the tyrannosaurus scrambled up again. The ground trembled and branches were ripped from nearby trees. All around the jungle had been leveled. Everything fell before the thrashing monsters.

Recovering, the snake's head darted in again, trying to circle the tyrannosaurus's head and complete the last and fatal coil, but the giant beast lunged, its massive jaws snapping, and the snake drew back. Suddenly its tail lashed out and circled the left legs of the tyrannosaurus. Astro could see the beast straining against the sudden pressure, at the same time alert for the swooping head of the snake. The pressure on the leg was too great, and the beast fell to the ground, giving the snake a momentary advantage. Its head darted in again, but the tyrannosaurus drew its head into its narrow shoulders, then shot out again as the snake missed. Astro saw the snake quiver and jerk back as the tyrannosaurus clamped its jaws closed and bit a chunk out of the green, scaly body.

The snake had enough. It wanted to get away, to slip to the top of the tallest tree in the forest, out of reach of the tyrannosaurus, and wait for the wound to heal or for death to come. It unwound in a maddened convulsive movement and slithered toward the tree where Astro lay. But the monster was after it, immediately grabbing it by the tail and jerking it back. The snake was forced to turn and fight back.

Astro knew that if the snake could get away it would head for the teakwood above his head, the highest tree around, and the tyrannosaurus would stamp the ground around its base into powder. He had to move!

A hundred feet to the left was a wild thicket of ground thorns, their needlelike tips bristling. Even the snake would stay away from them. It was his only chance should the snake get loose from the tyrannosaurus again. Making up his mind quickly, the cadet opened the end of the sleeping bag and shoved his weapons out before him. Then hugging the ground, he dashed across the clearing. This gave the tyrannosaurus its final advantage. The snake pulled back, momentarily attracted by Astro's move, and the tyrannosaurus struck, catching the snake just behind the head in a grip of death.

The thorns ripped at Astro's tight-fitting jungle dress, tearing into his flesh as he dove into the thicket. But once inside, the cadet lay still, pointing his rifle at the tyrannosaurus who was methodically finishing off the giant snake. In a few seconds the snake was dead and the tyrannosaurus began to feast.

Astro stayed in the thicket, watching the monster devour nearly all of the dead reptile foe and then rise up and move off through the jungle. Astro knew that in no time the scavengers of the jungle would be swarming over the remains of the snake. Once again he had to move.

Getting out of the thicket was painful. From every direction the thorns jabbed at him, and but for the toughness of his jungle suit, Astro would have been ripped to shreds. After easing his way back into the clearing, the cadet pulled out the remains of his jungle pack. He then saw that his suit was torn to ribbons, and the many slashes on his chest and arms were bleeding profusely. The scent of the blood would attract the carnivorous creatures, so he stripped off the bloody jungle suit, dropping it back in the thicket, and hurried away. A short time later he came to a water hole where he sponged himself off and applied medication from his emergency kit to the scratches. Finished, he took stock. The night's sleep had refreshed him, and except for the loss of his protective clothing, he was in good shape.

He shouldered the pack, strapped the paralo-ray gun to his hips, and gripping the rifle tightly, he moved off through the jungle once more. He decided to follow the tyrannosaurus. The beast would leave a path for him, saving him the effort of hacking his way through the vines and creepers, and should an enemy patrol be out, it would stay away from the tyrannosaurus. Finally, he knew Tom, Roger, and Connel would go after the beast if they saw it.

The sun shone down on the half-naked giant moving through the jungle, a new white-skinned animal who was braver than the rest, a creature who dared to trail the king of the jungle.

"IT'S ALL MY FAULT!" said Connel disgustedly. "I should have been able to read his trail signs."

Tom did not answer. He pulled the straps of his jungle pack tighter and slung it over his shoulder. Roger stood to one side, watching Major Connel. Both boys sensed what was coming.

"Well, this is the last day we can spend searching for

him," said Connel. "We've already lost two days."

Roger glanced at Tom and said casually, "It wouldn't hurt to keep our eyes open for signs of him, would it, sir?"

"Now listen, boys," said Connel firmly, "I know how you feel about Astro. I have to admit I have a liking for the lad myself. But we've been sent out here to locate the base of operations of the Nationalists. The best way to do that is to work around the jungle in a given area. We haven't done that so far. We've put all our time and effort into a random search for Astro. We can't signal him, build a fire, shoot off a blaster—or use any of the simple communication devices. We have to work under cover, for fear of giving away our presence here in the jungle." He slung his gear over his shoulder and added, "We'll continue our search for Astro until noon and then we simply will have to abandon it. And stop worrying about him. He's a big strong lad and he's been in this jungle alone before. I have every confidence that he can make his way back to Sinclair's plantation safely."

The Solar Guard officer paused and looked at the two downcast cadets before him. "None of that sulking business!" he growled. "You're cadets on an urgent mission. Now move out. I'll take the point first and you bring up the rear, Corbett." Without another word, the burly spaceman turned and moved off through the jungle.

Roger hung back to talk to Tom. "What do you think, Tom?"

Tom shook his head before answering. "He's right, Roger. We're on a job. It's the same here in the jungle as it is in space. We know that something is liable to happen to any one of us at any time. And the mission always comes first."

Roger nodded. "Sure, that's the way it is in the book. But this is real. That big hick might be hurt—or trapped. Maybe he needs our help!"

"I know how you feel, Roger," replied Tom. "I want to take off and hunt for Astro myself, but Connel needs us. Don't forget that bunch of guys in uniforms back at Sinclair's. Commander Walters and the others don't hold conferences like that one back in Venusport for the fun of it. This is serious."

Roger shrugged and started off after Connel, Tom following slowly behind. Their march through the jungle was made in silence, each hoping for a miracle. But as the sun grew higher and the deadline hour of noon approached, they steeled themselves to the fact that they might never see the Venusian cadet again. A short time later, when Tom was taking his turn at cutting the trail through the brush, he broke through into a clearing. He stopped and called out, "Major! Roger! Quick!"

Connel and the blond-haired cadet rushed forward, stopping beside Tom to stare in amazement. Before them, a large area of the jungle was pounded down, and lying amidst the tangle of giant creepers and uprooted bushes was the remains of a giant snake.

"By the rings of Saturn!" gasped Connel, walking forward to inspect the clearing. Tom and Roger followed, breaking to the side, their rifles at ready. The two boys had become jungle-wise quickly and knew that death lurked behind the wall of green surrounding the cleared area.

"It must have been some fight!" Connel pointed to the tracks of the tyrannosaurus. "The tyranno must have stumbled on the snake while it was feeding," said Connel. "Otherwise it would have lit out for that tree over there." He pointed to the giant teakwood that Astro had slept under. The three spacemen saw the makeshift sleeping bag at the same time.

"Major! Look!" cried Tom and raced to the base of the tree.

"It's Astro's, all right," said Connel, examining the woven bag. "I wonder if he was here when those two things were going after each other."

"Yes, sir," said Roger in a choked whisper, "he was." He pointed to the ragged remains of Astro's jungle suit dangling on the near-by thornbush. The blood was stiff on the material.

The three Earthmen stared at the suit, each too horrified to speak.

Connel's face was set in hard lines as he finally found his voice and growled, "Our search is over. Let's get back to our job."

11 IT WAS NOT UNTIL LATE THE SAME AFTERNOON THAT ASTRO, following the trail of the tyrannosaurus, realized that the giant beast was seriously hurt. At first the traces of blood on the ground and underbrush were slight, but gradually the blood spots became more profuse and the trail was covered with huge blotches of red. The Venusian cadet grew more cautious. The tyrannosaurus would be ten times as dangerous now. And it might be close by, lying in the jungle, licking its wounds.

As the sun began to sink in the western Venusian sky, Astro began to think about the coming night. He would have to hole up. He couldn't chance stumbling into the beast in the dark. But it would also mean taking time to make another sleeping bag. Suddenly he saw a movement in the brush to his left. He dropped to the ground and aimed the shock rifle in that direction, eyes probing the green tangle for further movement.

"Make one move and you'll die!" a harsh voice cut through the jungle. Astro remained still, his eyes darting to left and right, trying to locate the owner of the voice.

"Throw down your gun and stand up with your hands over your head!" came another voice, this one immediately behind him.

A patrol! Astro swore at himself for blindly walking into a trap and dropped his gun. He stood up and raised his hands over his head, turning slowly.

"Don't turn around! Stand still!"

Astro stopped.

He could hear the rustle of movement in the underbrush behind him and then someone called, "Circle around to the right. Spread out and see if there are any others!"

Off to the side, he could hear the crashing of footsteps moving away in the jungle.

"All right," continued the unknown voice, "drop that paralo-ray pistol to the ground. But no smart tricks. We can see you and you can't see us, so take it easy and do as we say."

Astro lowered his hands and unbuckled the gun belt, letting it fall to the ground. There was a sudden burst of movement behind him and powerful arms gripped his wrists. Within seconds his hands were tied quickly and expertly, and he was spun around to face his captors.

There were ten men, all dressed in the same green uniforms and plastic headgear he had seen at the Sinclair plantation. They stood in a semicircle around him, their guns leveled at his naked chest. The leader of the party nudged the nearest man and commented, "Never thought I'd see any animal like this in the jungle!" The other men laughed appreciatively.

"Who are you?" the leader demanded. "What are you doing here?"

"My name is Astro," replied the big cadet boldly. "I'm a Space Cadet, *Polaris* unit, Space Academy, U.S.A. I'm here in the jungle with the rest of my unit hunting tyrannosaurus."

"Tyranno, eh?" queried the man. "How long have you been trailing this one?"

"Just today. I saw him fight a big snake and lost my jungle gear in a thicket where I was hiding. I was separated from my space buddies two days ago."

"Say, Helia," suddenly called one of the other men, "he sounds like a Venusian."

"Is that true?" asked the leader. "Are you from Venus?"

Astro nodded. "Venusport."

"Then why are you in Space Academy?"

"I want to be a spaceman."

"Why didn't you go to school on Venus, instead of Earth. We have good space schools here."

"I want a commission in the Solar Guard. You can only get that through the Academy," replied Astro stoutly.

"Solar Guard!" snorted the leader, and then turned to the nearest man, speaking rapidly in a strange tongue.

For a moment the language confused Astro, then he recognized it as the ancient Venusian dialect. He understood it and started to answer, but then, on second thought, he decided not to reveal his knowledge of the language.

The leader turned back to Astro and asked a question.

Astro shook his head and said, "If you're talking to me, you have to speak English. I know that's the Venusian dialect you're speaking, but I never learned it."

The leader's fist shot out and crashed against Astro's jaw. The big cadet rocked back with the punch and then he lunged forward, straining against his bonds.

"Why, you—!" he exploded angrily.

"That was for not being a true Venusian!" snapped the leader. "Every son of Venus should understand his mother tongue!"

Astro bit his lip and fell silent.

The leader turned away, and shouting a command, started off through the jungle. Astro knew that the patrol had been ordered to move out, but he stood still, waiting for them to push him. They did. A hard jab in his naked side with the butt of a gun sent him stumbling forward in the center of the patrol.

Well, there was one consolation, he thought grimly. At least he wouldn't have to spend the night out in the jungle alone again!

Astro had expected a long march, but to his surprise, he was pushed along a well-worn jungle trail for only three hundred yards in from the tyrannosaurus's track. Finally they stopped before a huge teakwood tree. The leader pounded his rifle butt on the trunk three times.

Mystified, Astro watched a small section of the trunk open to reveal a modern vacuum-tube elevator shaft. He was pushed inside with the men of the patrol and the tree-trunk door was closed. The leader pushed a lever and the car dropped so suddenly that Astro nearly lost his balance. He judged that they must have fallen two hundred feet when the car stopped and another door opened. He was pushed out into a high-vaulted tunnel with cement walls.

"Hurry up!" snapped the leader.

The big cadet moved along the tunnel, followed by the patrol, turning from one tunnel into another, all of them slanting downhill. Astro guessed that he was being taken to some subterranean cave. He asked his captors where they were taking him.

"Don't talk!" snapped one of the men at his side.

"This jungle will be swarming with Solar Guardsmen once they discover I'm lost," said Astro. "Who are you and what are you holding me prisoner for?" The big cadet decided it would be better to feign ignorance of the existence of the rebel organization.

"Let the Solar Guard come!" snapped the leader. "They'll find something they never expected."

"But what do you want with *me*?" asked the cadet.

"You'll know soon enough!"

They had been walking for nearly an hour and the tunnels still slanted downward but more sharply now. Turning into a much larger tunnel than any of the rest, Astro noticed a huge door on one side. Through its crystal-covered ports he saw racks of illegal heat blasters and paralo-ray guns. A man stepped out of the door, and raising his hand in a form of salute, called out a few words in the Venusian tongue. Astro recognized it as a greeting, "Long live Venusians!" and suppressed a smile.

One by one, the men of the patrol handed over their rifles and ray guns, while the man in the armory checked off their names. Then they all removed their knee-length jungle boots and traded their plastic helmets for others of the same design but of a lighter material. Each man turned his back while switching helmets, obviously to avoid being recognized by any of the others, since the new helmet was also frosted except for a slit at eye level. Wearing the lighter headgear and common street shoes, the men continued their march through the tunnel. They passed into a still larger tunnel, and for the first time, Astro could see daylight. As they drew nearer to the mouth of the tunnel, the cadet could see outside, and the scene before him made him gasp for breath.

A full twenty miles long and fifteen miles wide, a canyon stretched before him. And it seemed to the big cadet that every square inch of the canyon floor was occupied by buildings and spaceships. Hundreds of green-clad men were moving around the ships and buildings.

"By the craters of Luna!" gasped Astro as the patrol

paused in the mouth of the tunnel. "What—what is this?"

"The first city of Venus. True Venus. Built by Venusians with Venusian materials only!" said the leader proudly. "There's the answer to your Solar Guard!"

"I don't understand," said Astro. "What are you going to do?"

"You'll see." The man chuckled. "You'll see. Move on!"

As they trooped out of the tunnel and down into the canyon they passed groups of men working on the many ships. The cadet recognized what they were doing at once. The unmistakable outlines of gun ports were being cut into the sides of several bulky space freighters. Elsewhere, the steady pounding of metal and grinding of machinery told the cadet that machine shops were going at full blast. He noticed a difference between the men of the patrol and the workers. Neither spoke to the other. In fact, Astro saw that it was rarely that a worker even glanced at them as they passed by.

Up ahead, Astro saw a huge building, wide and sprawling but only a few stories high. It was nearly dark now and lights began to wink on in the many windows. He guessed that he was being taken to the building and was not surprised when the leader pulled him by the arm, guiding him toward a small side door. There was a curious look about the building and the cadet couldn't figure out what it was. Glancing quickly at the wall as he passed through the door, he nearly burst out laughing. The building was made of wood! He guessed that the rebels were using materials at hand rather than importing anything from outside planets. And since Venus was largely a planet of jungles and vegetation, with few large mineral deposits, wood would be the easiest thing to use.

The inside of the building was handsomely decorated and designed. He saw walls covered with carvings, depicting old legends about the first colonists. He shook his head. "Boy," he thought, "they sure go for the Venusian stuff in a big way!"

"All right!" snapped the leader. "Stop here!"

Astro stood before a huge double door that had been polished to a brilliant luster. The cadet waited for the leader to enter, but the Nationalist stood perfectly still, eyes straight ahead. Suddenly the doors swung open, revealing a huge chamber, at least a hundred and fifty feet long. At the far end a man dressed in white with a green band across his chest sat in a beautifully carved chair. Arrayed on either side of him were fifty or more men dressed in various shades of green. The man in white lifted his hand and the patrol leader stepped forward, pushing Astro before him. They walked across the polished floor and stopped ten feet away from the man in white, the patrol leader bowing deeply. Astro glanced at the men standing at either side of the man in white. The bulge of paralo-ray pistols was plainly visible beneath their flowing robes.

The man in white lifted his hand in the salute Astro had seen before. Then the patrol leader straightened up and began to speak rapidly in the Venusian dialect. Translating easily, Astro heard him report his capture. When he concluded, the man in white looked at Astro closely and spoke three words. Astro shook his head.

"He does not speak our mother tongue, Lactu," volunteered the patrol leader.

The man in white nodded. "How is it," he said in English, "that you are a native-born Venusian and do not speak the language of your planet?"

"I was an orphan. I had very little formal education," said Astro. "And as long as we're asking questions around here, how about my asking a few? Who in space are you? What's the idea of holding me a prisoner?"

"One question at a time, please, brother Venusian," said the man in white. "And when you address me, my name is Lactu."

"Lactu what?" asked Astro belligerently.

"Your own name should tell you that we on Venus only have one name."

"Never mind that rocket wash!" barked Astro. "When do I get out of here?"

"You will never leave here as you came," said Lactu quietly.

"What does that mean?" demanded the cadet.

"You have discovered the existence of our base. Ordinarily you would have been burned to a crisp and left in the jungle. Fortunately, you are a Venusian by birth, and therefore have the right to join our organization."

"What does that mean?"

"It means," said Lactu, "that you will take an oath to fight until death if necessary to free the planet Venus and the Venusian citizens from the slavery of the Solar Alliance and—"

"Awright, buster!" roared Astro. "I've had enough of that rocket wash! I took an oath of allegiance to the Solar Guard and the Solar Alliance, to uphold the cause of peace throughout the universe and defend the liberties of the planets. Your idea is to destroy peace and make slaves out of the people of Venus—like these dummies you've got here!" Astro gestured contemptuously at the men standing on both sides of Lactu. "I don't want any part of you, so start blasting!" continued the big cadet, his voice booming out in the big room. "But make it good, 'cause I'm tough!"

There was a murmur among the men and several put their hands on the butts of their paralo-ray guns. Even the calm expression in Lactu's eyes changed.

"You are not afraid of us, are you?" he asked in a low, almost surprised tone of voice.

"You, nor anything that crawls in the jungle like you!" shouted Astro. "If you're not happy with the way things are run on Venus, why don't you take your beef to the Solar Alliance?"

"We prefer to do it our way!" snapped one of the men near Lactu. "And as for you, a few lashes with a Venusian wet whip will teach you to keep a civil tongue!"

Astro turned around slowly, looking at each of the men individually. "I promise you," he said slowly, "the first man who lays a whip on me will die."

"And who, pray, will do the killing?" snorted a short, stout figure in the darkest of the green uniforms. "You? Hardly!"

"If it isn't me"—Astro turned to face the man—"it will be any one of a thousand Space Cadets."

"You have a lot of confidence in yourself and your friends," said Lactu. "Death apparently doesn't frighten you."

"No more than it does any man of honor," said the cadet. "I've faced death before. As for my friends"—Astro shrugged and grinned—"touch me and wait for what happens. And by the stars, mister, you can depend on it happening!"

"Enough of this, Lactu!" said a man near the end of the group. "We have important business to conduct. Take this foolish boy out and do away with him!"

Lactu waved his hand gently. "Observe, gentlemen, here is the true spirit of Venus. This boy is not an Earthman, nor a Martian. He is a Venusian—a proud Venusian who has drifted with the tides of space and taken life where he found it. Tell me honestly, gentlemen, what would you have thought of Astro, a Venusian, if he had acted any differently than he has? If he had taken an oath he does not believe and groveled at our feet? No, gentlemen, to kill this proud, freeborn Venusian would be a crime. Tell me, Astro, do you have any skills?"

"I can handle nuclear materials in any form."

"We are wasting time, Lactu!" exclaimed one of the men suddenly. "Settle with this upstart later. Now let us take a vote on the issue before us. The ship is waiting to blast off for Mercury. Do we ask for her assistance, or not?"

There was a loud murmur among the assembled men, and Lactu held up his hand. "Very well, we will vote. All in favor of asking the people of Mercury to join our movement against the Alliance will say aye!"

"Aye," chorused the men.

"Against?"

Lactu looked around, but there was no reply.

Lactu turned back to Astro. "Well, Venusian, this is your last chance to join forces with us and to fight for your mother planet."

"Go blast your jets!" snapped Astro. Immediately Lactu's eyes became hard steely points.

"That was your last chance!" he said. "Take him out and kill him!"

The door suddenly burst open and a green-clad trooper raced across the bare floor, bowing hastily before Lactu.

"Forgive this interruption, Lactu," he said breathlessly.

"There are men in the jungle headed for the canyon rim. Three of them!"

Lactu turned to Astro. "Your friends, no doubt!" He snapped an order. "Capture them and bring them to me. And as for you, Astro, we are in need of capable men to build war heads for our space torpedoes. To ensure the safety of your friends, I would advise your working for us. If not, your friends will die before another night falls."

12 "YOU'RE RIGHT, TOM," SAID MAJOR CONNEL. "They must be around here somewhere. Start looking. If they're not here, it may mean he's still alive."

It was Tom who had thought of looking for Astro's weapons. Refusing to believe that his unit mate had been killed, the curly-haired cadet was examining the torn jungle suit when the idea occurred to him.

Quickly Roger, Connel, and Tom spread out over the trampled area, searching the underbrush for Astro's paralo-ray pistol or shock rifle. Connel examined the underbrush and vines closely for scorch marks made by the blaster. Finding none, he rejoined the boys.

"Well?" he asked.

"Nothing, sir," replied Roger.

"Can't find them, Major," said Tom.

Connel smacked his fists together and spoke excitedly. "I'm sure Astro wouldn't be caught unawares by a couple of things like a snake or a tyrannosaurus without putting up a fight. If he was attacked suddenly, he would have fired at least one shot, and if it went wild, it would have burned the vines and brush around here. You didn't find his weapons, and there are no scorched areas. I'll stake my life on it, Astro's alive!"

Roger's and Tom's faces brightened. They knew Connel had no proof, but they were willing to believe anything that would keep their hopes for their giant unit mate alive.

"Now," said Connel, "assuming he is not dead, and that he is somewhere in the jungle, we have to figure out what he would do."

Roger was thoughtful a moment. "How long would he last without his jungle suit, sir?"

"What do you mean?" asked Connel.

Tom's eyes lit up. "If he's alive, sir, then he's probably following a path or trail that would keep him away from heavy underbrush," he said.

Connel thought a moment. "There's only one trail away from here." He turned and pointed to the trail made by the tyrannosaurus. "That one."

The three spacemen stared at the wide path left by the huge beast. Connel hesitated. "It's due north," he said finally. "We've come a full day west and should be making a turn north. We'll follow the tyrannosaurus's trail for a full day."

Roger and Tom grinned. They knew Connel was making every effort to find Astro, while still keeping his mission in mind.

The three spacemen moved along the trail quickly, eyes alert for any sign Astro might have left. Connel saw the great bloodstains left by the tyrannosaurus and cautioned the two cadets. "This tyranno is wounded pretty badly. It might be heading back for its lair, but it might not make it, and stop along the way. Be careful and keep your eyes open for any sign that he might have—"

Connel was stopped by Tom's sudden cry. "Major! Look!"

Connel turned and stared. A thousand yards ahead of them on the broken trail they saw the monstrous bulk of a tyrannosaurus emerge from the gloom.

"By the rings of Saturn," breathed Connel, "that's the one!"

The great beast spotted the three Earthmen at the same instant. It raised itself on its hind legs, and shaking its massive head in anger, started to charge down its own trail toward them.

"Disperse!" cried Connel. "Take cover!"

Tom and Roger darted to one side of the trail while Connel dived for the other. Taking cover behind a tree, the boys turned and pointed their rifles down the trail. They saw that the tyrannosaurus had already covered half the distance between them.

"Aim for the legs!" shouted Connel, from his place of concealment. "Don't try for a head shot! He's moving too fast! Give it to him in the legs. Try to cut him down!"

Roger and Tom lay flat on the ground and trained their rifles on the approaching beast.

"I'll take the right leg," said Roger. "You take the left, Tom."

"On target!" replied Tom, squinting through the sight.

"Ready!" Connel's voice roared across the trail.

Only a hundred and fifty feet away the tyrannosaurus, hearing Connel's voice,

suddenly stopped. Its head weaved back and forth as though it suspected a trap.

"Fire!" roared Connel.

Tom and Roger fired together, but at the same moment the monster lunged toward Connel's position. Both shots missed, the energy charges merely scorching its sides.

The tyrannosaurus roared with anger and turned toward the boys, head down and the claws of its short forelegs extended.

At that moment Connel opened fire, aiming for the monster's vulnerable neck. But it was well protected behind its shoulders and the spaceman only succeeded in drawing the beast's attention back to himself.

At this instant Tom and Roger opened fire again, sending violent shock charges into the beast's hide. Caught in the withering cross fire, it turned blindly on the boys and charged at them. The two cadets fired coolly, rapidly, unable to miss the great bulk. The air became acrid with the sharp odor of ionized air. Maddened now beyond the limits of its endurance, hit at least twenty times and wild with pain, the great king of the Venusian jungle bore down on the two cadets.

Roger and Tom saw that their fire was not going to stop the tyrannosaurus's charge. They were pouring a nearly steady stream of fire into the monster now, while on the other side of the trail Connel was doing the same, raking the monstrous hulk from the forelegs to the hindquarters.

The boys jumped back, Tom still facing the beast and firing his rifle from the waist. But Roger stumbled in the tangle of the underbrush and fell backward, dropping his rifle. The beast's head swooped low, jaws open.

Seeing Roger's danger, Tom jumped downward again without hesitation and fired point-blank at the beast's scaly head, only ten feet away.

The monster roared in sudden agony and pulled back, jerking his head up against a thick branch of the tree overhead. The limb tore loose under the impact and fell crashing to the ground on top of Roger.

From behind, Connel stepped closer to the tyrannosaurus and fired from a twenty-five-foot range. It wavered and stumbled back, obviously mortally wounded. From both sides Tom and Connel poured their weapons' power into the giant beast. Blinded, near death, the monster wavered uncertainly. Bellowing in fear and pain, it turned and lumbered back down the trail.

Connel and Tom watched it until they were certain it could not attack them without warning again, and then they hurried to Roger. The heavy tree limb had landed across his back, pinning him to the ground.

"Roger!" yelled Tom. "Roger, are you all right?"

The blond-haired cadet didn't answer. Grabbing a stout branch lying on the ground nearby, Connel and Tom worked it beneath the limb which lay across Roger's body and pried it up.

"I've got it," said Connel, holding the weight of the limb on his shoulder. "Pull him out!"

Tom quickly pulled the unconscious cadet clear and laid him on the ground. Dropping the limb, Connel bent down to examine the boy. He ran his fingers along Roger's spine, feeling the bones one by one through the skin-tight jungle suit. Finally he straightened and shook his head. "I can't tell anything," he said. "We'll have to take him back to Sinclair's right away." He stood up. "I'll make a stretcher for him. Meanwhile, you go after that tyranno and finish him off. He's pretty far gone, but you never can tell."

"Aye, aye, sir," replied Tom. He picked up his rifle and reloaded it, checking it carefully. He repeated the precaution with Roger's blaster.

"Hurry up," urged Connel, already reaching for a suitable branch. "Time means everything now."

"Be right back, sir," replied Tom. And as he walked away, he looked back at the unconscious form of his unit mate. He could not help reflecting on the bitter fact that already two members of the expedition were in danger, and they were no closer to their goal of finding the Nationalists' hidden base.

Moving carefully, one of the two rifles slung over his shoulder, the other in his hand ready for use, Tom followed the trail of the tyrannosaurus. Two thousand yards farther along he saw a place where the monster had fallen and then struggled back to its feet to stagger on. Rounding a turn in the trail, Tom stopped abruptly. Before him, not a hundred feet away, the beast lay sprawled on the ground. The area all around was devoid of any vegetation. It was trampled down to the black soil. Tom deduced that it was the beast's lair. He pressed forward cautiously until he was a scant thirty feet away, and crouched between the roots of a huge tree where he would be protected should the monster be able to rise and fight again.

Sighting carefully on the base of the monster's neck, he squeezed the trigger of the shock rifle. A full energy charge hit the tyrannosaurus in its most vulnerable spot. It jerked under the sudden blast, involuntarily tried to rise to its feet, and then fell back, the ground shaking under the impact of its thirty tons. Then, after one convulsive kick with its hind legs that uprooted a nearby tree, the beast stiffened and lay still.

Tom waited, watching the beast for signs of life. After five minutes he stepped forward cautiously, his rifle ready. He circled the tyrannosaurus slowly. The great bulk towered above him, and the cadet's eyes widened in amazement at the size of the fallen giant. Stopping at its head, which was as wide as he was tall, Tom looked at the jaws and teeth that had torn so many foes into bloody bits, and shook his head. He had come to the jungle to kill just such a beast. But with Astro missing and Roger unconscious, the thrill of victory was somehow missing. He turned and headed back down the trail.

Connel had finished the litter by the time Tom returned, and the officer was leaning over the blond-haired cadet, examining his back again.

"We'd better move out right away, Tom," said Connel. "I still can't tell what's wrong. It may be serious, and then it may be nothing more than just shock. But we can't take a chance."

Tom nodded. "Very well, sir." He adjusted his shoulder pack, slung both rifles over his shoulder, and started to pick up his end of the litter when suddenly the jungle silence was shattered by a deafening roar. Connel jumped to his feet!

"Corbett!" he cried. "That's a rocket ship blasting off!"

"It sure sounded like it, sir," replied Tom.

"And I'll stake my life it's not more than a half mile away!"

The two men jumped out into the trail and scanned the sky. The unmistakable roar of a spaceship echoed through the jungle. The ship was accelerating, and the reverberations of the rocket exhaust rolled over the treetops. Suddenly a flash of gleaming metal streaked across the sky and Connel roared.

"We've found it, Corbett!" He slapped the cadet on the back. "The Nationalists' base! We've found it!"

Tom nodded, a half-smile on his face. "We sure have, Major." He hesitated a moment. "You know, sir, if Roger is really badly hurt we might not make it back to Sinclair's in time, so—" He stopped.

"I know what you're thinking, Tom," said the officer, "and I agree. But one of us has to go back with the information."

"You go, sir," said Tom. "I'll take Roger and—"

"You can't carry him alone—"

"I can make it somehow," protested Tom.

Connel shook his head. "I'll help you."

"You mean, you're going to allow yourself to be captured too?" spluttered Tom.

"Not quite." Connel smiled. "But a good intelligence agent gets as much information as he can. And he gets correct information! I'll help you get him to the base and you can take him on in for medical attention. I'll get back to Sinclair's later."

Tom tried to protest, but the burly spaceman had turned away.

13 "STAND WHERE YOU ARE!"

Tom and Major Connel stiffened and looked around, the unconscious form of Roger stretched between them on the litter. From the jungle around them, green-clad Nationalists suddenly emerged, brandishing their guns.

"Put Roger down," muttered Connel quietly. "Don't try anything."

"Very well, sir," replied Tom, and they lowered the litter to the ground gently.

"Raise your hands!" came the second command from a man who appeared directly in front of them.

Standing squarely in front of them, the little man said

something in the Venusian dialect and waited, but Connel and Tom remained silent.

"I guess you don't speak the Venusian tongue," he sneered. "So I'll have to use the disgusting language of Earth!" He looked down at the unconscious form of Roger. "What happened to him?"

"He was injured in a fight with a tyrannosaurus," replied Connel. "May I remind you that you and these men are holding guns on an officer of the Solar Guard. Such a crime is punishable by two years on a prison asteroid!"

"You'll be the one to go to prison, my stout friend!" The man laughed. "A little work in the shops will take some of that waistline off you!"

"Are you taking us prisoner?"

"What do you think?"

"I see." Connel seemed to consider for a moment. "Who are you?" he asked.

"I am Drifi, squad officer of the jungle patrol."

"Connel, Senior Officer, Solar Guard," acknowledged Connel. "If we are being held prisoner, I wish to make a request."

"Prisoners don't make requests," said Drifi, and then added suspiciously, "What is it?"

"See that this man"—Connel indicated Roger—"is given medical attention at once."

Drifi eyed the major cautiously.

"I make this request as one officer to another," said Connel. "A point of honor between opponents."

Drifi's eyes gleamed visibly at the word *officer*, and Tom almost grinned at Connel's subtle flattery.

"You—and you," snapped Drifi at the green-clad men around them, "see that this man is taken to the medical center immediately!" Two men jumped to pick up the litter.

"Thank you," said Connel. "Now will you be so kind as to tell me what this is all about?"

"You'll find out soon enough. We have a special way of treating spies."

"Spies!" roared Connel. The officer sounded so indignant that Tom was almost fooled by his tone. "We're hunters! One of our party is lost here in the jungle. We were searching for him when we were attacked by a tyranno-saurus. During the fight, this man was injured. We're not spies!"

Drifi shrugged his shoulders, and barking a command to his men, turned into the jungle. Connel and Tom were forced to follow.

They were taken to the giant teakwood that Astro had seen, and Tom and Connel watched silently as the door opened, revealing the vacuum tube. The men crowded into the car and it dropped to the lower level.

Following the same twisting turns in the tunnels, Tom and Connel were brought to the armory and saw the men surrender their weapons and change their helmets and shoes. They tried desperately to get a look at the faces of the men around them while the headgear was being changed, but, as before, the men were careful to keep their faces averted.

Continuing down the tunnel, Connel tried to speak to Drifi again. "I would appreciate it greatly, sir," he said in his most formal military manner, "if you could give me any news about the other man of our party. Have you seen him?"

Drifi did not answer. He marched stiffly ahead, not even bothering to look at Connel.

As they neared the exit, Connel drifted imperceptibly closer to Tom and whispered out of the side of his mouth, "Keep your eyes open for ships. Count as many as you can. How many are armed, their size, and so on. Look for ammunition dumps. Check radar and communications installations. Get as much information as you can, in case only one of us can escape."

"Yes, sir," whispered Tom. "Do you think they might have Astro?"

"It's a good guess. We were following the tyrannosaurus's trail when they caught us, and I'm pretty sure Astro had been doing the same thing."

"Stop that talking!" snapped Drifi, suddenly whirling on them. "You," he shouted at one of the guards, "get up here and keep them apart!"

A guard stepped quickly between Tom and Connel, and the conversation ended.

At the exit Connel and Tom stopped involuntarily at the sight before them. Astro had entered the canyon near twilight, but the two spacemen got a view of the Nationalists' base under the full noon sun. Connel gasped and muttered a space oath. Tom turned halfway to his superior and was starting to speak when both were shoved rudely ahead. "Keep moving," a guard growled.

As they walked, their eyes flicked over the canyon, alert for details. Tom counted the ships arrayed neatly on the spaceport some distance away, then counted others outside repair shops with men scurrying over them like so many ants. Near the center of the canyon the bare trunk of a giant teakwood soared skyward, a gigantic communications tower. Tom scanned the revolving antenna, and from its shape and size deduced the power and type of radar being used at the base. He admitted to himself that the Nationalists had the latest and best. Connel was busy too, noting buildings of identical design scattered around the canyon floor that were too small to be spaceship hangars or storage depots. He guessed that they were housings for vacuum-tube elevator shafts that led to underground caves.

The canyon echoed with the splutter of arc welders, the slow banging of iron workers, the cough and hissing of jet sleds, the roar of activity that meant deadly danger to the Solar Alliance. Connel noticed as he moved across the canyon floor that the workers were in good spirits. The morale of the rebels, thought the space officer, was good! Too good!

At a momentary halt in their march, when Drifi stopped to speak with a sentry, Tom and Connel found an opportunity to speak again.

"I've counted a dozen big converted freighters on the blast ramps, sir," whispered Tom hurriedly. "Three more being repaired, nearly finished, and there are about fifty smaller ships, all heavily armed."

"That checks with my count, Tom," replied Connel hurriedly. "What do you make of the radar?"

"At least as good as we have!"

"I thought so, too! If a Solar Guard squadron tried to attack this base now, they'd be spotted and blasted out of space!"

"What about stores, sir?" asked Tom. "I didn't see anything like a supply depot."

Connel told him of the small buildings which he believed housed the elevator shafts to underground storerooms. "Only one thing is missing!" he concluded.

"What's that, sir?"

"The nuclear chambers where they produce ammunition for their fleet."

"It must be underground too, sir," said Tom. "There isn't a building in the canyon that's made of concrete and steel."

"Right. Either that, or it's back up there in the cliffs in one of those tunnels!" The officer snorted. "By the stars, Corbett, this place is an atom bomb ready to go off in the lap of the Solar Alliance."

"What are we going to do, sir?" asked Tom. "So far, it looks as if it's going to be tough to get out again."

"We'll have to wait for a break, Tom," sighed Connel.

"I hope they've taken good care of Roger," said the cadet in a low voice. "And I hope they've got Astro."

"Watch it," warned Connel. "Drifi's coming back. Remember, if we're separated and you do manage to escape, get back to Sinclair's. Contact Commander Walters and tell him everything that's happened. The code name for direct emergency contact through Solar Guard communications center in Venusport is Juggernaut!"

"Juggernaut!" repeated Tom in a whisper. "Very well, sir. But I sure hope we aren't separated."

"We'll have to take what comes. *Sh!* Here he comes."

"All right, let's go," said the patrol leader.

They continued across the canyon until they reached a four-story wooden structure without windows. Drifi opened a small door and motioned them inside.

"What is this?" Connel demanded.

"This is where you'll stay until Lactu sends for you. Right now, he is in conference with the Division Leaders."

"Divisions of what? Ships? Men?" asked Connel offhandedly, trying not to show any more than idle curiosity.

"You'll find out when the Solar Guard comes looking for a fight," said Drifi. "Now get in there!"

Tom and Connel were shoved inside and the door closed

behind them. It was pitch black, and they couldn't see an inch in front of their faces. But both Tom and Connel knew instantly that they were not alone.

"COME ON. GIMME THAT WRENCH!" barked Astro. The little man beside him handed up the wrench and leaned over the side of the engine casing to watch Astro pull the nut tight. "Now get over there and throw on the switch," snapped the big cadet.

The little man scurried over to one side of the vast machine shop and flipped on the wall switch. There was an audible hum of power and then slowly the machine Astro had just worked on began to speed up, soon revving up to ten thousand revolutions per minute.

"Is it fixed?" demanded the shop foreman, coming up beside Astro.

"Yeah, she's fixed. But I don't work on another job until you give me another helper. That asteroid head you gave me doesn't know a—" Astro stopped. Something out beyond the double doors caught his eye. It was the sight of Tom and Connel entering the wooden building.

"What's the matter with him?" demanded the foreman.

"Huh? What? Oh—ah—well, he's OK, I guess," Astro stammered. "It's just that he's a little green, that's all."

"Well, get to work on that heater in chamber number one. It's burned a bearing. Change it, and hurry up about it!"

"Sure—sure!" The big cadet grinned.

"Say, what's the matter with you?" asked the foreman, staring at him suspiciously.

"I'm OK," replied Astro quickly.

The foreman continued to stare at Astro as the big cadet turned to his assistant nonchalantly. "Come on, genius, get that box of tools over to the heater!" he shouted. As he turned away, the foreman nodded to the green-clad guard, who followed closely behind Astro, his hand on the butt of his paralo-ray gun.

Seeing the little assistant struggling with the heavy box, Astro stopped and picked it out of his arms with one hand. Grinning, he held it straight out and then slowly brought it around in a complete circle over his head, still holding it with only one hand. The guard's eyes widened behind his plastic helmet at this show of strength.

"You're very strong, Astro," he said, "but you are altogether too contemptuous of a fellow Venusian." He nodded to the small assistant.

"That's right," said Astro. His grin hardened and he leaned forward slightly, balancing on the balls of his feet. "That goes for you and every other green space monkey in this place. Drop that ray gun and I'll tie you up in a knot!"

Frightened, the guard pulled the paralo-ray gun out of its holster, but Astro quickly stepped in and sank his fist deep into the guard's stomach. The man dropped like a stone. Astro grinned and turned his back to walk toward the heater. He heard the other workers begin to chatter excitedly, but he didn't pay any attention to them.

"Astro! Astro!" His little assistant ran up beside him. "You hit a division guard!"

"I did, huh?" replied the big cadet in an innocent tone. "What kind of a division?"

"Don't you know? Venus has been divided into areas called divisions. Each division has a chief, and every Venusian citizen in that division is under his personal jurisdiction."

"Uh-huh," said Astro vaguely. He climbed up onto the machine and began taking off the outer casing.

"The best men in the division are made the Division Chief's personal guards."

"What happens to the second and third and fourth best men?"

"Well, they're given jobs here according to their knowledge and capacities."

"What was your job before you came here?"

"I was a field worker on my chief's plantation."

"Why did you join?" asked Astro. "Did you think it better to have Venusians ruling Venus, instead of belonging to the Solar Alliance?"

"I didn't think about it at all," admitted the little man. "Besides, I didn't join. I was recruited. My chief just put me on a ship and here I am."

"Well, what do you think of it, now that you're here?"

asked Astro. He began running his fingers along a few of the valves, apparently paying no attention to the guard who was just now staggering to his feet.

The little assistant paused and considered Astro's question. Finally he replied weakly, "I don't know. It's all right, I guess. It's better here in the shops than in the caves where the others go."

"Others? What others?"

"Those that don't like it," replied the man. "They're sent to the caves."

"What caves?"

"Up in the cliff. The tunnels—" He suddenly stopped when an angry shout echoed in the machine shop. The guard Astro had hit rushed up. He turned to several workmen nearby. "Take this blabbering idiot to the caves!" he ordered angrily.

Astro slowly climbed down from the machine and faced the guard menacingly. As the guard's finger tightened on the trigger of his paralo-ray gun, the foreman suddenly rushed up and knocked the gun out of his hand. "You fool! You stiffen this man and we'll be held up in production for hours!"

"So what!" sneered the guard.

"Lactu and your Division Chief will tell you so what!" barked the foreman. He turned to Astro. "And as for you, if you try anything like that again, I'll—"

"You won't do a thing," said Astro casually. "I'm the best man you've got and you know it. Lactu knows it too. So don't threaten me and keep these green space jerks away from me! I'll fix your machines, because I want to, not because you can make me!"

The foreman eyed the big cadet curiously. "Because you want to? You've changed your tune since you first came here."

"Maybe," said Astro. "Maybe I like what I see around here. It all depends."

"Well, make up your mind later," barked the foreman. "Now get that machine fixed!"

"Sure," said Astro simply, turning back to the machine and starting to whistle. Strangely enough, he was happy.

He was a prisoner, but he felt better than he had in days. Just knowing that Tom and Major Connel were right across the canyon gave him a surge of confidence. Working over the machine quickly, surely, the big cadet began to formulate a plan. Now was the time! They were together again. Now was the time to escape!

14 **"PUT YOUR BACK AGAINST THE DOOR, TOM!"** snapped Connel. "Quickly!"

Tom felt the powerful grip of the Solar Guard officer's fingers on his arm as he was pulled backward. He closed his eyes, then opened them, hoping to pierce the darkness, but he saw nothing. Beside him, he could sense the tenseness in Connel's body.

There was a rustle of movement to the right of them.

"Careful, Tom," cautioned Connel. "To your right!"

"I hear it, sir," said Tom, turning toward the noise and bracing himself.

"My name is Connel," the burly spaceman suddenly spoke up in loud tones. "I'm an official in the Solar Guard! Whoever you are, speak up! Identify yourself."

There was a moment of silence and then a voice spoke harshly in the darkness.

"How do we know you're a Solar Guard officer? How do we know you're not a spy?"

"Do you have any kind of light?" asked Connel.

"Yes, we have a light. But we are not going to give away our positions. We know how to move in here. You don't."

"Then how do you expect me to prove it?"

"The burden of proof lies with you."

"Have you ever heard of me?" asked Connel after a pause.

"We know there is an officer in the Solar Guard named Connel."

"I am that officer," asserted Connel. "I was sent into the

jungle to find this base, but one of our party was injured and we were captured by a patrol."

Tom and Connel heard voices whispering in the darkness and then a loud order.

"Lie down on the floor, both of you!"

The two spacemen hesitated and then got down flat on their backs.

"Close your eyes and lie still. One of us here knows what Connel looks like. I hope for your sake that you're telling the truth. If you're not—" The voice stopped but the threat was plain.

"Do as they say, Tom," said Connel.

The cadet closed his eyes and he heard the shuffle of feet around them. Suddenly there was a flash of light on his face but he kept his eyes tightly closed. The light moved away, but he could tell that it was still burning.

"It's Connel, I think," said a high-pitched voice directly over them.

"Are you sure?"

"Pretty sure. I met him once in Atom City at a scientific meeting. He was making a speech with a Professor Sykes."

"That's right," said Connel, hearing the remark. "I was there."

"Do you remember meeting a man from Venus wearing a long red robe?" asked the high-pitched voice.

Connel hesitated. "No," he said. "I only remember talking to three men. Two were from Venus and one was from Mars. But neither of the two from Venus wore a red robe. They wore purple—"

"He's right," acknowledged the voice. "This is Connel."

"Open your eyes," said the first voice.

Connel and Tom opened their eyes and in the light of a small hand torch they saw two gaunt faces before them. The tallest of the men stuck out a bony hand. "My name is Carson." They recognized his voice as the one that had spoken first. "And this is Bill Jensen," he added.

"This is Tom Corbett, Space Cadet," said Connel. He glanced around the room, and in the weak reflected light of the torch, saw almost fifty men crouched against the walls, each of them holding a crude weapon.

"You'll understand our caution, Major," said Carson. "Once before we had a plan to escape and a spy was sent in. As you see, we didn't escape."

"Neither did the spy," commented Jensen grimly.

"How long have you been here?" asked Connel.

"The oldest prisoner has been here for three years," replied Carson. And as the other men began to gather around them, Connel and Tom saw that they were hardly more than walking skeletons. Their cheeks were hollow, eyes sunk in their sockets, and they wore little more than rags.

"And there's no way to escape?" asked Tom.

"Three guards with blasters are stationed on the other side of that door," said Carson. "There is no other entrance or exit. We tried a tunnel, but it caved in and after that they put in a wooden floor." He stamped on it. "Teak. Hard as steel. We couldn't cut through."

"But why are you being held prisoners?" asked Connel.

"All of us joined the Nationalists believing it was just a sort of good-neighbor club, where we could get together and exchange ideas for our own improvement. And when we found out what Lactu and the Division Chiefs were really up to, we tried to quit. As you see, we couldn't. We knew too much."

"Blasted rebels!" muttered Connel. "The Solar Guard will cool them off!"

"I'm afraid it's too late," said Carson. "They're preparing to strike now. I've been expecting it for some time. They have enough ships and arms to wipe out the entire Solar Guard garrison here on Venus in one attack!" He shook his head. "After that, with Solar Guard ships and complete control of the planet—" He paused and sighed. "It will mean a long, bloody space war."

Tom and Connel plied the prisoners with questions and soon began to get a complete picture of the scope of the Nationalist movement.

"Lactu and his commanders should be sent to a prison asteroid for life," said Carson, "for what they have done to former Nationalists."

"Hundreds of unsuspecting Venusians have been brought here under the guise of helping to free Venus. But when they come and recognize what Lactu really intends to do, they want to quit. But it's too late, and they're sent to the caves."

Tom looked at the gaunt man fearfully. There was something in his voice that sent a chill down his spine.

"They are driven like cattle into the canyon walls," continued Carson. "There they are forced to dig the huge underground vaults for storage dumps. They are beaten and whipped and starved."

"Why aren't you in the caves then?" asked Connel.

"Some of us were," replied Carson. "But each of us here owns land and it is necessary to keep us alive to send back directives to our bankers and foremen to give aid in one form or another to Sharkey and the Division Chiefs."

"I see," said Connel. "If you were to die, then your property would be out of their reach."

"Exactly," said Carson.

"Is Sharkey the real leader of the movement?"

"I don't believe so. But then, no one knows. That's the idea of the frosted helmets. If you don't know who a man is, you can liquidate him without conscience. He may be your closest friend, but you would never know it."

"The blasted space crawlers!" growled Connel. "Well, they'll pay!"

"You have a plan?" asked Carson eagerly.

"No," said Connel slowly, "but at least we all have more of a chance now."

"How?" asked Carson.

"The Solar Guard sent us here to find this base. If we don't return, or send some sort of message back within a reasonable time, this jungle will be swarming with guardsmen!"

Carson looked a little disappointed. "We shall see," he said.

THERE WERE THREE THINGS ON ASTRO'S MIND as twilight darkened into night over the canyon. One, he had to find out why Roger wasn't with Tom and Connel when they were taken into the building; two, he had to figure out a way to contact Tom and Connel; and finally, he had to escape himself, or help Tom and Connel escape.

The big cadet finished the last job in the machine shop. It had taken very little time, but the big cadet had lingered over it, trying to find answers to his three problems. Around him, the workers were leaving their benches and lathes, to be replaced by still others. A twelve-hour shift was being used by the Nationalists in their frantic preparations for an attack on the Venusport garrison of the Solar Guard. Astro finally dropped the last wrench into the tool kit and straightened up. He stretched leisurely and glanced over at his guard. The man was still rubbing his stomach where Astro had hit him, and he watched the big cadet with a murderous gleam in his eye.

"All finished," said Astro. "Where and when do I eat?"

"If I had my way, you wouldn't," sneered the guard.

"Either I knock off and eat," said Astro confidently, "or I call the foreman and you talk to Lactu."

"Feeling pretty big, aren't you?" growled the guard. "I haven't forgotten that punch in the stomach."

"Why, I hardly touched you," said Astro in mock surprise.

The guard glared at him, muttered an oath, and turned away. Astro could see that he was boiling, almost out of his mind with helpless, frustrated anger, and suddenly the young cadet realized how he would be able to move about the base freely. Grinning, he walked arrogantly in front of the guard and out of the shop into the dark Venusian night. It was very warm and many of the workers had stripped down to their trousers. He passed the open doorway of a large tool shop and glanced inside. It was empty. The men had apparently gone to eat. He suddenly stopped, turned to the guard, and growled, "If you want to settle our differences now, we can step inside."

The guard hesitated and glared at Astro. "When I settle with you, big boy, you'll know about it."

"What's the matter with right now?" asked Astro. "Yellow?" He turned and walked into the tool shop without looking back. The guard rushed after him. But the big cadet had carefully gauged the distance between them, and when he heard the rushing steps of the guard immediately behind him, he suddenly spun around, swinging a roundhouse right, catching the guard in the pit of the stomach again. The man stopped dead in his tracks. His eyes bulged and glazed, and he dropped to the floor like a stone. Astro pulled the man to the corner of the empty shop, removed the plastic helmet, and then tied and gagged him. He pulled the helmet over his own head, nearly tearing one ear off, grabbed the gun and stepped back outside. He stood in front of the door and glanced up and down the area between the  buildings. Fifty feet away a group of men were working over a tube casing, but they didn't even look up.

Staying in the shadows, he walked down the lane, moving carefully. The plastic helmet would keep him from being recognized right away, but to complete his plan, he needed one of the green uniforms of the guards.

Deciding it would be too risky to walk around the base, he crouched behind a huge crate of machinery at the head of the lane. Sentries were constantly patrolling the area and he was certain that one would pass by soon. He only hoped the man would be big enough. Fifteen minutes later the cadet heard footsteps in a slow measured tread. He peered around the edge of the crate and silently breathed a thankful prayer. It was a green-clad guard, and luckily, almost as big as he was.

Crouching in the shadow of the crate, Astro tensed for the attack. It had to be quick and it had to be silent. He couldn't club the guard because of his helmet. He would have to get him around the throat to choke off any outcry.

The slow steps came nearer and the big cadet raised himself on the balls of his feet, ready to spring. When the guard's shadow fell across him, Astro leaped forward like a striking tiger.

The guard didn't have a chance. Astro's arm coiled around his throat and the cry of alarm that welled up within him died down in a choking gasp. Within seconds he was unconscious and the big cadet had dragged him behind the crate. He stripped him of his uniform, bound and gagged him with his own rags, and crammed him into the crate. Then, protected by the helmet and green uniform and carrying the blaster, the cadet stepped out confidently and strode down the lane.

He went directly to the building he had seen Tom and Connel enter, and walked boldly up to the guard lounging in front of the door.

"You're relieved," said Astro in the Venusian dialect. "They want you up in the caves." The cadet had no idea where the caves were, but he knew that they couldn't be nearby and it would be some time before an alarm could be sounded.

"The caves?" asked the guard. "Who said so?"

"The chief. He wants you to identify somebody."

"Me? Identify someone? I don't understand." The guard was puzzled. "What section of the caves?"

"The new section," said Astro quickly, figuring there must be a new and an old section because he had heard a guard refer to the old one.

"Up by the jungle tunnels?"

Astro nodded.

"Must be more of those Solar Guardsmen," said the guard, relaxing. "We have two of them in here, another in the hospital, and one of them working in the machine shop."

Hospital! Astro gulped. That would be Roger. But he dared not ask too many questions. "What's going to happen to them?" he asked casually.

"I don't know," said the guard, "but I wish we'd hurry up and attack Venusport. I'm getting tired of living out here in the jungle."

"Me too," said Astro. "Well, you'd better get going."

The guard nodded and started to walk away. Suddenly Astro stiffened. Two other guards were rounding the corner of the building. He called to the departing guard quickly. "Who's on duty with you tonight?"

"Maron and Teril," replied the guard, and then strode off into the darkness.

"So long," said Astro, turning to face the two men walking toward him. He would have to get rid of them.

"Hello, Maron, Teril," he called casually. "Everything quiet?"

"Yes," replied the shorter of the two, as they stopped in front of Astro, "no trouble tonight."

"Well, there's trouble now!" growled Astro. He brought up the blaster and cocked it. "Make one wrong move, and you're dead little space birds! Get over there and open that door!"

Stunned, both men turned to the door without a protest and Astro took their guns. "Open up!" he growled.

The men slid the heavy bar back and pushed the door open.

"Get inside!" ordered Astro. The two men stumbled inside. Astro stepped to the door. "Tom! Major!"

There was a cry of joy from the blackness within and Astro recognized Tom.

"Astro!" roared Connel, rushing up. "What in the stars—?"

"Can't talk now," said Astro. "Here. Take these blasters and then tie these two up. Close the door, but leave it open a crack. We can talk while I stay outside and keep watch. If there isn't a guard out here, it might mean trouble."

"Right," said Connel. He took the blasters, tossing one over to Tom. "Blast it, I never felt anything so good in my life!" He closed the door, leaving it open an inch.

"Why is Roger in the hospital?" asked Astro quickly.

Connel told him of the fight with the tyrannosaurus and Roger's injury, ending with their capture by the patrol.

"You know what's going on here, Major?" asked Astro.

"I sure do," said Connel. "And the sooner we blast them, the happier I'll be."

"One of us will have to escape and get back to the *Polaris* to contact Commander Walters," said Astro. "But they've got radar here as good as ours. That has to be put out of commission or they can blast any attacking fleet."

"You're right," said Connel grimly, and turned back into the room. "Tom!" he called.

"Yes, sir," replied Tom, coming up to the door.

"Since Astro and I speak Venusian—" said Connel, and then added when Tom gasped, "Yes, I speak it fluently, but I kept it a secret. That means you're the one to go. Astro and I will have more of a chance here. You escape and return to the *Polaris*. Contact Commander Walters. Tell him everything that's happened. We'll give you thirty-six hours to make it. At exactly noon, day after tomorrow, we'll knock out their radar."

"But how, sir?" asked Tom.

"Never mind. We'll figure out something. Just get back to the *Polaris* and tell the Solar Guard to attack at noon, day after tomorrow. If you don't and the fleet attacks earlier, or later, they'll be wiped out."

"What about you, sir?" asked Tom.

"If you get back in time, we'll be all right. If not, then this is good-by. We'll hold out as long as we can, but that can't be forever. We're fighting smart, determined men, Tom. And it's a fight to the finish. Now hurry up and get into one of those uniforms."

While Tom turned back inside to put on the uniform, Connel returned to Astro outside the door. "Think we can do it, Astro?"

"I don't see why not, sir," replied the big cadet.

A moment later Tom returned, dressed in one of the guard's green uniform and wearing a helmet. Carson was with him, similarly clad. "Astro better show me the way out of the base," said Tom. "Carson will stand guard until he gets back."

"Good idea," said Connel. Tom and Carson slipped out the door.

"All set, Astro?" asked Tom.

"Yeah, there's only one thing wrong," replied the big cadet.

"What's the matter?" asked Connel.

"I don't know the way out of the base."

15

"I CAN TELL YOU THE WAY OUT OF THE BASE."
Adjusting the plastic helmet over his head, Carson stepped up close to Astro and Tom and spoke confidently. "It's very simple."

"Whew!" exclaimed Tom. "I thought we'd have to go fumbling around."

Carson pointed through the darkness. "Follow this lane straight down until you come to a large repairlock. There's a space freighter on the maintenance cradle outside. You can't miss it. Turn left and follow a trail to the base of the canyon wall. There are jungle creepers and vines growing up the side and you can climb them easily."

Tom nodded and repeated the directions, then turned to Astro. "Maybe you'd better stay here, Astro. I can make it alone."

"No." Connel spoke sharply from the doorway. "Astro speaks Venusian. If you're stopped, he can speak for you. You'd give yourself away."

"Very well, sir," said Tom. "I guess that is best. Ready to go, Astro?"

"Ready," replied the big cadet.

"Good-by, Major," said Tom, reaching into the doorway to shake hands with Connel. "I'll try my best."

"It's a matter of life and death, Tom." Connel's voice was low and husky. "Not our lives, or the lives of a few people, but the life and death of the Solar Alliance."

"I understand, sir." Tom turned to Astro and the two cadets marched off quickly.

They had no difficulty finding the giant ship on the cradles outside the repair shop and quickly turned toward the base of the cliff. Twenty minutes later they had left the center of activity and were close to the canyon wall. They were congratulating themselves on their luck in not being stopped or questioned when suddenly they saw a guard ahead of them on sentry duty.

"I'll take care of him," whispered Astro. "You hide here in the shadows, and when I whistle, you start climbing. Then I'll cover you from there until you get to the top. Got it?"

"Right!" The two cadets shook hands briefly. Each knew that there was no need to speak of their feelings.

"Take care of Roger," said Tom. "We don't know how badly he's been injured."

"I'll see to him," said Astro. "Watch me now and wait for my whistle." He turned away and then paused to call back softly, "Spaceman's luck, Tom."

"Same to you, Astro," replied Tom, and then crouched tensely in the shadows.

The big cadet walked casually toward the sentry, who spotted him immediately and brought his gun up sharply, calling a challenge in the Venusian tongue.

"A friend," replied Astro in the same dialect.

The sentry lowered the gun slightly. "What are you doing out here?" he asked suspiciously.

"Just taking a walk," said Astro. "Looking for something."

"What?" asked the sentry.

"Trying to make a connection."

"A connection? What kind of connection?"

"This kind!" said Astro suddenly, chopping the side of his hand down on the sentry's neck, between the helmet and his uniform collar.

The sentry fell to the ground like a poleaxed steer and lay still. Astro grinned, then turned and went whistling off into the darkness. Twenty feet away Tom heard the signal and hurried to the base of the cliff. He grabbed a thick vine and pulled himself upward, hand over hand. Halfway up he found a small ledge and stopped to rest. Below him, he could see Astro hurrying back toward the center of the base. The dim lights and the distant hum of activity assured him that so far his escape was unnoticed. He resumed his climb, and fifteen minutes later the curly-haired cadet stood on the canyon rim. After another short rest he turned and plunged into the jungle.

Tom knew that as long as he kept the planet of Earth over his right shoulder, while keeping the distant star of Regulus ahead of him, he was traveling in the right direction to Sinclair's plantation. He stopped to check his bearings often, occasionally having to climb a tree to see over the top of the jungle. He ignored the threat of an attack by a jungle beast. For some reason it did not present the danger it had when he had first entered the jungle, seemingly years before. Under pressure, the cadet had become skilled in jungle lore and moved with amazing speed. He kept the blaster ready to fire at the slightest movement, but fortunately during the first night he encountered nothing more dangerous than a few furry deerlike animals that scampered behind him off the trail.

Morning broke across the jungle in a sudden burst of sunlight. The air was clear and surprisingly cool, and Tom felt that he could make the Sinclair plantation by nightfall if he continued pushing full speed ahead.

He stopped once for a quick meal of the last of the synthetics that he had stuffed in his pocket from his shoulder pack, and then continued in a steady, ground-eating pace through the jungle. Late in the afternoon he began to recognize signs of recent trail blazing, and once he cut across the path Astro had made. He wondered if the trail was one Astro had cut while he was lost, or previously. He finally decided to go ahead on his own, since he had managed to come this far without the aid of any guide markers.

As the darkening shadows of night began to spread over the jungle the young cadet began to worry. He had been allowed thirty-six hours to make it back to the *Polaris*, communicate with Commander Walters, and tell him the position of the base, and Tom had to allow time for the Solar Guard fleet to assemble and blast off, so that it would arrive at the base at exactly noon on the next day. He had to reach the Sinclair plantation before nightfall or the fleet would never make it.

Suddenly to his left he heard a noisy crashing of underbrush and the roar of a large beast. Tom hesitated. He could hide; he could fight; or he could break to his right and try to escape. The beast growled menacingly. It had picked up his scent. Tom was sure it was a large beast on the prowl for food, and he decided that he could not waste time hiding, or risk being injured in a battle with the jungle prowler. He quickly broke to his right and raced through the jungle. Behind him, the beast picked up the chase, the ground trembling with its approach. It began to gain on him. Tom was suddenly conscious of having lost his bearings. He might be running away from the clearing!

Still he ran on, legs aching and lungs burning. He charged through the underbrush that threatened any moment to trip him. When he was almost at the point of complete exhaustion, and ready to turn and face the beast behind him, he saw something that renewed his spirit and sent new strength through his body. Ahead through the vines and creepers, the slender nose of the *Polaris* was outlined against the twilight sky.

Disregarding the beast behind him, he plunged through the last few feet of jungle undergrowth and raced into the clearing around the Sinclair home. Behind him, the beast suddenly stopped growling, and when Tom reached the airlock of the *Polaris*, he saw that the beast had turned back, reluctant to come out of the protection of the jungle.

Tom pulled the air-lock port open and was about to step inside when he heard a harsh voice coming from the

shadow of the port stabilizer.

"Just stop right where you are!"

Tom jerked around. Rex Sinclair stepped out of the shadow, a paralo-ray gun in his hand.

"Mr. Sinclair!" cried Tom, suddenly relieved. "Boy, am I glad to see you!" He jumped to the ground. "Don't you recognize me? Cadet Corbett!"

"Yes, I recognize you," snarled Sinclair. "Get away from that airlock or I'll blast you!"

Tom's face expressed the confusion he felt. "But, Mr. Sinclair, you're making a mistake. I've got to get aboard and warn—" He stopped. "What's the idea of holding a paralo ray on me?"

"You're not warning anybody!" Sinclair waved the gun menacingly. "Now get over to the house and walk slowly with your hands in the air or I'll freeze you solid!"

Stunned by this sudden turn of events, Tom turned away from the airlock. "So you're one of them, too," said Tom. "No wonder we were caught in the jungle. You knew we were looking for the base."

"Never mind that," snapped Sinclair. "Get into the house and make it quick!"

The young cadet walked slowly toward the house. He saw the charred remains of the burned outbuildings and nodded. "So it was all an act, eh? You had your buildings burned to throw us off the track. Small price to pay to remain in the confidence of the Solar Guard."

"Shut up!" growled Sinclair.

"You might be able to shut me up, but it'll take a lot more than a bunch of rabble rousers to shut up the Solar Guard!"

"We'll see," snapped Sinclair.

They reached the house and Tom climbed the steps slowly, hoping the planter would come close enough for a sudden attack, but he was too careful. They moved into the living room and Tom stopped in surprise. George Hill and his wife were tied hand and foot to two straight-backed chairs.

Tom gasped. "George! Mrs. Hill!"

George Hill strained against his bonds and mumbled something through the gag in his mouth, but Tom couldn't understand what he was trying to say. Mrs. Hill just looked at the planter with wide, frightened eyes. The cadet whirled around angrily. "Why, you dirty little space rat!"

Sinclair didn't hesitate. He squeezed the trigger of his paralo-ray gun and Tom stiffened into rigidity.

The planter dropped the ray-gun into a chair and leisurely began to tie the hands and feet of the immobilized cadet.

"Since you can hear me, Corbett," said Sinclair, "and since you are powerless to do anything about what I'm about to tell you, I'm going to give you a full explanation. I owe it to you. You've really worked for it."

Unable to move a muscle, Tom nevertheless could hear the planter clearly. He mentally chided himself at his stupidity in allowing himself to be captured so easily.

Sinclair continued, "My original invitation to you and your friends, to use my home as a base for your hunting operations was sincere. I had no idea you were in any way connected with the investigation the Solar Guard was planning to make into the Nationalist movement."

Tom was completely bound now, and the planter stepped back, picked up the ray-gun, and flipping on the neutralizer, released the cadet from the effects of the ray charge. Tom shuddered involuntarily, his nerves and muscles quivering as life suddenly flowed into them again. He twisted at the bonds on his wrists, and to his amazement found them slightly loose. He was sure he could work his hands free, but decided to wait for a better opportunity. He glanced at the clock on the wall nearby and saw that it was nine in the evening. Only fifteen hours before the Solar Guard must attack!

Sinclair sat down casually in a chair and faced the cadet. George and Mrs. Hill had stopped struggling and were watching their employer.

"Do you know anything about the bomb we found on the *Polaris* on our trip to Venus?" asked Tom.

"I planned that little surprise myself, Corbett," said Sinclair. "Unfortunately our agents on Earth bungled it."

"It seems to me that was pretty stupid. There would have been another man sent in Major Connel's place, and we were warned that something big was in the wind."

"Ah, quite so, Corbett," said Sinclair. "But the destruction of the *Polaris* would have caused no end of speculation. There would have been an investigation which would have temporarily removed the spotlight from the Nationalist movement. That would have given us ample time to complete our preparations for the attack."

"Then you knew," said Tom bitterly, "when Major Connel, Roger, Astro, and I left here that we were going to be captured."

"Well, that was one of the details of the final plan. Personally, I hoped that you and your nosy major would meet a more dramatic and permanent end in the jungle."

"What are you going to do with us?" asked Tom, glancing at George and his wife. "And what do Mr. and Mrs. Hill have to do with your scheme?"

"Unfortunately they discovered who I am, and of course had to be taken care of. As to your eventual disposition, I haven't had time to think about that."

"Well, you'd better start thinking," said Tom. "And you'd

better do a good job when you attack the Solar Guard. Perhaps you don't know it, Sinclair, but the whole pattern of the Solar Guard is one of defense. We do not invite attack, but are prepared for it. And we have the power to counterattack!"

"When we get through with your Solar Guard, Corbett," sneered Sinclair, "there won't be anything left but smoldering heaps of junk and the dead bodies of stupid men!"

The buzz of a teleceiver suddenly sounded in another part of the house and Sinclair left the room quickly. When he was sure the planter was out of earshot, Tom turned to George and whispered, "I think I can work my hands loose. Where can I find a ray-gun?" George began to mumble frantically but Tom couldn't understand him, and the sound of returning footsteps silenced Hill. The planter strode back into the room, hurriedly putting on the green uniform of the Nationalists. "I've just received word of a speed-up in the preparations for our attack," he said. "Soon, Corbett—soon you will see what will happen to the Solar Guard!"

16 "BRING THAT DIRTY LITTLE SPACE CRAWLER IN HERE!"

Captain Strong had never seen Commander Walters so angry. The cords stood out in his neck and his face was red with fury as he paced up and down the Solar Guard office in Venusport. "A spy," he roared. "A spy right in the heart of our organization!" He shook his head.

The door opened and two burly Solar Guardsmen entered, saluted, and turned to flank the doorway, hands on their paralo-ray pistols. The private secretary of E. Philips James shuffled in slowly, followed by two more guards. Walters stepped up to the thin, intense young man and glared at him. "If I had my way, I'd send you out to the deepest part of space and leave you there!"

The man bit his lip but said nothing.

"Where is your secret base?" demanded Walters.

"I don't know," replied the secretary nervously.

"Who told you to intercept this message from Mercury?" Walters tapped a paper on his desk. "Who gave you your orders?"

"I receive orders on an audioceiver in my home," answered the man, a slight quaver in his voice. "I have never seen my superior."

"And you followed the Nationalist movement blindly, doing whatever they told you, without question, is that it?"

"Yes."

"Yes, *sir!*" roared Walters.

"Yes, sir," corrected the secretary.

"Who told you to forge those orders for priority seats on the *Venus Lark*?"

"My superior," said the man.

"How did you know Major Connel was coming here to investigate the Nationalists?"

"I read the decoded message sent to the Solar Delegate, Mr. James."

"Who told you to send men to bomb the *Polaris*?"

"My superior," said the man.

"Your superior—your superior!" Walters' voice was edged with contempt. "What else has your superior told you to do?"

"A great many things," said the young man simply.

Walters studied the thin face and then turned to Captain Strong. "There's only one thing to do, Steve. There's no telling how many of these rats are inside our organization. Relieve every civilian in any position of trust and put in our own man. I'll make a public televiewer broadcast in half an hour. I'm declaring martial law."

"Yes, sir," replied Strong grimly.

"If you hadn't been in the code room when this message from Mercury came in, we would never have known the Nationalists were trying to get the Mercurians to join them in their attack on us until it was too late. It's the only break we've had, so far, learning that the Mercurians are still decent, loyal Solar citizens. I hate to think of what would have happened if they hadn't warned us."

"He very nearly got away with it, sir," said Strong. "If I hadn't heard the signal for a top-secret message come through on the coding machine, I never would have suspected him. He tried to hide it in his tunic. He also confessed to trying to kidnap the cadets when he heard me tell them that a cab would be waiting for them."

"Well, we know now," said Walters. He turned to one of the guardsmen. "Sergeant, I'm holding you personally responsible for this man."

"Aye, aye, sir," said the guard, stepping toward the secretary, but Walters stopped him and addressed the man.

"I'll give you one last chance to tell me where your base is and how many ships you have," he said.

The secretary looked down at his feet and mumbled, "I don't know where the base is, and I don't know how many ships there are."

"Then what does this list we found in your tunic mean?" snapped Strong. "These are the names of ships that have been lost in space."

"I don't know. That list was sent to me over the audioceiver by my superior. I was to relay it to Mercury should they accept our proposal to join forces against—" He stopped.

"Get him out of my sight!" barked Walters.

The guards closed in around the little man and he slowly shuffled out of the office.

"I wonder how many more there are like him in our organization, Steve?" The commander had turned to the window and was staring out blindly.

"I don't know, sir," replied Strong. "But I think we'd better be prepared for trouble."

"Agreed," said Walters, turning to the Solar Guard captain. "What do you suggest?"

"Since we don't know how many ships they have, where their base is, or when they plan to attack, I suggest putting the Venus squadrons in defense pattern A. Meanwhile, call in three additional squadrons from Mars, Earth, and Luna. That way, we can at least be assured of an even fight."

"But we don't know if they'll attack here on Venus. Suppose we weaken Earth's fleet and they attack there?" Walters paused, looking troubled. Then he sighed. "I guess you're right. Put the plan into effect immediately. It's the only thing we can do."

At exactly midnight every teleceiver on Venus was suddenly blacked out for a moment and then came into focus again to reveal the grim features of Commander Walters.

In homes, restaurants, theaters, arriving and departing space liners, in every public and private gathering place, the citizens of Venus heard the announcement.

"As commander in chief of the Solar Guard, I hereby place the entire planet of Venus under martial law. All public laws are suspended until further notice. All public officials are hereby relieved of their authority. A ten P.M. until six A.M. curfew will go into effect immediately. Anyone caught on the streets between these hours will be arrested. An attack is expected on the city of Venusport, as well as other Venusian cities, momentarily. Follow established routine for such an occurrence. Obey officers and enlisted men of the Solar Guard who are here on Venus to protect you and your property. That is all!"

IN THE LIVING ROOM OF SINCLAIR'S HOUSE Tom waited impatiently for the sound of Sinclair's yacht taking off before attempting to free himself from the rope on his wrists. But when a half-hour had passed with no sound from outside, he decided not to waste any more time.

Relaxing completely, the curly-haired cadet began working his wrists back and forth in the loop of rope. It was slow, painful work, and in no time the skin was rubbed raw. George and Mrs. Hill watched him, wide-eyed. They saw the skin of his wrists gradually turn pink, then red, as the cadet pulled and pushed at the rope. A half-hour had passed before he felt the rope slipping down over the widest part of his hand. Slowly, so as not to lose the precious advantage, he pulled with all his strength, unmindful of the pain. He heard a sharp gasp from Mrs. Hill and then felt the rope become damp. His wrists were bleeding. But at the same time he felt the rope slipping over his hands. He gave a quick tug and the rope slipped off and dropped to the floor, a bloody tangle. He spun around and untied the foreman and his wife quickly, removing the gags from their mouths gently.

"Your wrists!" cried Mrs. Hill.

"Don't worry about them, ma'am," said Tom. He looked at Hill. "How long have you been tied up?"

"Just about an hour before you came," answered the foreman. "I found Sinclair in front of a teleceiver in his room. It's in a secret panel and I didn't know it was there. I waited and heard him talking to someone in Venusian. But he spotted me and pulled a ray-gun."

"Do you know where he's gone?" asked Tom.

"No, but I sure wish I did!" said the burly foreman stoutly. "I have something to settle with him."

"That'll have to wait until the Solar Guard is finished with him. Come on!" Tom started toward the door.

"Where are we going?" asked Hill.

"To the *Polaris*! I've got to warn the Solar Guard of their plans. They're going to attack the Venusport garrison and take over Venus!"

"By the stars!" gasped Mrs. Hill. "Here I've been feeding that man all these years and didn't know I was contributing to a revolution!"

Tom was out of the door and running toward the *Polaris* before she had finished talking. George followed right behind him.

As the cadet raced across the dark clearing one hope filled his mind—that the *Polaris* would be in the same condition in which they had left it.

The port was still open where Sinclair had caught him, and he climbed inside the giant ship quickly. As soon as he entered, he snapped on the emergency lights and searched the ship carefully. After examining every compartment, and satisfied that there was no one aboard, he made his way back to the radar bridge. There, he saw immediately why Sinclair had felt free to leave the ship. All radar and communications equipment had been completely smashed.

The young cadet returned to the control deck and called down to George Hill, waiting in the airlock. "George! Get Mrs. Hill aboard quickly. We're blasting off!"

"Blasting off?" the foreman called back. "But I thought you were going to contact Venusport!"

"I can't," replied Tom. "Sinclair has smashed the communications and the radar. We'll have to take our information to Venusport in person. I only hope he's left the rockets and atomic motors alone."

"How about using the teleceiver in the house?" asked the foreman, climbing up to the control deck.

"Can't take a chance," said Tom. "This is top secret. They might have the teleceiver tapped."

"Do you know how to handle this ship alone?" asked George, glancing around at the great control board. "I don't know anything about a ship this size."

"I can handle it," said Tom. "Get Mrs. Hill aboard!"

"Here I am, Tommy," said Mrs. Hill, climbing up into the control deck. "I have some bandages and salve for your wrists."

"There's no time, Mrs. Hill," said Tom. "We've got to—"

"Nonsense!" she interrupted firmly. "You just give me your hands. It'll take only a minute!"

Tom reluctantly held out his wrists and Mrs. Hill expertly applied the salve and bandaged the cadet's raw wrists. Admittedly feeling better, Tom turned to the master switch and found it missing. For a second panic seized him, until he remembered that Major Connel had hidden it. He felt under the pilot's chair and breathed easier, pulling out the vital instrument.

"Better get into acceleration chairs," said Tom, strapping himself into his seat. "This might be a rough take-off."

"Watch yourself, Tom," cautioned George. "We aren't afraid for ourselves, but you've got to get to Venusport!"

"If he's left the power deck alone, everything will be OK."

The young cadet stretched out a trembling hand and switched on the automatic firing control. Then, crossing his fingers, he flipped on the main generator and breathed easier as the steady hum surged through the ship. He thought briefly of Astro and Roger, wishing his two unit mates were at their stations, and then switched on the power feed to the energizing pumps. There was a second's wait as the pressure began to build, and he watched the indicator over his head on the control panel carefully. When it had reached the proper level, he switched in the reactant feed, giving it full D-12 rate. He glanced at the astral chronometer over his head automatically and noted the time.

"Stand by!" he called. "Blast off minus five—four—three—two—one—*zero!*"

He threw the master switch and a roaring burst of power poured into the main tubes. The ship bucked slightly, raised itself from the ground slowly, and then suddenly shot upward. In less than a minute the *Polaris* had cleared atmosphere and Tom turned on the artificial-gravity generators. He made a quick computation on the planetary calculator, fired the port steering rockets, and sent the ship in a long arching course for Venusport. Then, unstrapping himself, he turned to see how Mr. and Mrs. Hill had taken the blast-off.

The foreman and his wife were shaking their heads, still in acceleration shock, and Tom helped them out of their cushions.

"Oh, my! Do you boys have to go through this all the time?" Mrs. Hill asked. "It's a wonder to me how a human body can take it."

"I feel pretty much the same way," muttered George.

"A cup of hot tea will fix you up fine," Tom reassured them, and leaving the ship on automatic control, he went into the small galley off the control deck and brewed three cups of tea. In a few moments the elderly couple felt better, and Tom told them of the Nationalists' base and Connel's plan to wreck the radar station at noon the next day. Both Mr. and Mrs. Hill were shocked at the scope of the Nationalists' plan.

"Well, they bit off more than they could chew when they decided to buck the Solar Guard," asserted Tom. "When Commander Walters gets finished with them, Sinclair and the rest won't have anything left but memories!"

"Tell me something, Tom," said George, looking at the control panel thoughtfully. "Have you figured out how you're going to land this ship alone and with no radar?"

"I'll have to use the seat of my pants." Tom smiled, and turned back to his seat. George and his wife looked at each other and quickly strapped themselves into their acceleration cushions.

A few moments later Tom began braking the ship with

the nose rockets. It made a slow-climbing arc over the spaceport and then settled slowly, tailfirst. The stern teleceiver was out of order, and the young cadet had to rely entirely on "feel," to get the *Polaris* in safely. He had calculated his rate of fall, the gravity of Venus, and the power of the rockets, and was dropping at a predetermined rate. At the critical point he increased power on the drive rockets, continuing to fall slowly until he felt the jarring bump of the directional fins touching the ground.

"Touchdown!" he roared triumphantly.

He closed the master switch and turned to look at the smiling faces of Mr. and Mrs. Hill.

"That was fine, Tom," said George, "but I don't want to do it again."

"Don't be a scaredy cat, George Hill!" taunted Mrs. Hill. "Tom handles this ship as if he were born on it."

Tom grinned. "We'd better hurry up. There must be something going on. There aren't any lights on here at the spaceport and all the administration buildings are dark."

He hurried to the airlock and swung it open, jumping lightly to the ground.

"Halt!" growled a rough voice. "Get your hands in the air and stay right where you are!"

Puzzled, Tom did as he was told, announcing, "I'm Space Cadet Tom Corbett, *Polaris* unit. I request immediate transportation to Commander Walters. I have important information for him."

He was momentarily blinded by the glare of a ring of lights around him, and when he finally could see, he found himself in the middle of a squad of Solar Guardsmen in battle dress.

"What's the password?" asked a tough sergeant whose shock rifle was aimed right at Tom's midsection.

"Juggernaut!" replied Tom quietly.

The word sent the sergeant into a frenzy of action. "Peters, Smith, get the jet car around here!"

"What's up, Sergeant?" asked Tom. "Why is everything so dark?"

"Martial law!" replied the guardsman. "Curfew from ten until six."

"Whew!" gasped Tom. "It looks as if I just made it!"

As George and Mrs. Hill climbed out of the airlock, a jet car raced up and skidded to a stop in front of them. A moment later Tom and the couple, accompanied by two of the guardsmen, were speeding through the dark and empty streets of Venusport. The car was stopped once at a mid-town check point, and Tom had to repeat the password. They picked up another jet car, full of guardsmen as escorts, and with the echo of the exhausts roaring in the empty avenues, they sped to central Solar Guard headquarters.

Tom had never seen so many enlisted guardsmen in one spot before, except on a parade ground. And he noted with a tinge of excitement that each man was in battle dress. Arriving at headquarters, they were whisked to the top floor of the building and ushered into Commander Walters' office. The commander smiled broadly as the young cadet stepped to the front of his desk and saluted smartly.

"Cadet Corbett reporting, sir," he said.

In a moment the office was filled with men; E. Philips James, the Solar Delegate, Captain Strong, fleet commanders, and officers of the line.

"Make your report, Cadet Corbett," said Walters.

Tom spoke quickly and precisely, giving full details on the location of the base, the approximate number of fighting ships, the armament of each, the location of supply dumps, and finally of Major Connel's plan to sabotage the radar at noon the following day. Then, one by one, each official asked him questions pertinent to their tasks. Fleet commanders asked about the ships' speed, size, armor; Strong inquired about the stores and supporting lines of supply; Walters asked for the names of all people connected with the movement. All of these questions Tom answered as well as he could.

"Well, gentlemen," said Walters, "thanks to Corbett and the others on this mission, we have all the information we need to counter the Nationalists. I propose to follow Major Connel's plan and attack the base at noon tomorrow. Squadrons A and B will approach from the south and east at exactly noon. Squadrons C, D, and E will come in from the north and west as a second wave at 1202. The rest of the fleet will go in from above at 1205. Supporting squadrons are now on their way from Earth and Mars. Blast off at six hundred hours. Spaceman's luck!"

"Good work, Tom," said Strong, when the conference broke up.

"Yes, sir," said Tom. "But I can't help worrying about Roger and Astro and Major Connel. What's going to happen to them, sir?"

Strong hesitated. "I don't know, Tom. I really don't know."

17 "WHAT TIME IS IT, ASTRO?"

"Exactly eleven o'clock, sir."

"All set?"

"Yes, sir."

"You know what to do. Move out!"

Astro and Major Connel were crouched behind a pile of fuel drums piled near the communications and radar building in the heart of the Nationalists' base. Above them, the gigantic tree used as the radar tower rose straight into the Venusian morning sky.

After helping Tom to escape, Astro had returned to the prison building for Connel and was surprised to find the place surrounded by green-clad Nationalist guards. Rather than attempt to release Connel then, Astro hid and waited for the time set to wreck the radar communications of the enemy. During the second day, he had successfully eluded the many patrols looking for him. Once from a hiding place he overheard one of the men mention Connel. He took a daring chance and approached the patrol openly. Speaking the Venusian dialect, he learned that Connel had escaped. That news sent the cadet on a different game of hide-and-seek as he prowled around the base searching for the Solar Guard officer. He had found him hiding near the radar tower, and they spent the night close to the communications building waiting for the time to strike.

Their plan was simple. Astro would enter the building from the front, while Connel would enter from the rear. Astro would draw attention to himself, and while the guards inside the building were busy dealing with him, Connel would come upon them from behind, knock them out of action, and then destroy the radar equipment.

The two spacemen gave no thought to their own safety. They were concerned only with accomplishing their objective. Having no way of knowing whether Tom had made it back to Venusport or whether their destruction of the communications center would be of any value, they nevertheless had to proceed on the assumption that Tom had gotten through.

Astro crawled behind the drums and stopped twenty feet from the door to wait for several Nationalist officers to leave. They finally got into a jet car and roared away. Astro nodded to the major waiting to edge around to the rear and then headed for the main entrance.

Connel saw Astro making his way to the front door and hurried around to complete his part of the mission. He waited exactly three minutes, gripped his shock rifle firmly, and then crossed over to the rear of the building and stepped inside.

Once inside, the major found it difficult to keep from bursting into laughter. The large ground-floor room was a frenzy of brawling, yelling, shouting Nationalist guards trying to capture the giant cadet. Astro was standing in the middle of the floor, swinging his great hamlike fists methodically, mowing down the guards like tenpins. Two of them were on his back, trying to choke him, while others crowded in from all sides. But they could not bring the cadet down. Astro saw Connel, shook himself, and stood free.

"Stand back!" roared Connel. "The first one of you green monkeys that makes a move will have his teeth knocked out! Now line up over there against the wall—and I mean fast!"

The sudden attack from the rear startled the Nationalist guards, and they milled around in confusion. There was no confusion, however, when Connel fired a blast over their heads. Astro grabbed a paralo-ray gun and opened up on the guards. A second later the squad of Nationalists were frozen in their tracks.

Once the men were no further danger to them, Connel

and Astro locked the front and rear doors and then raced up the stairs that led to the main radar and communications rooms on the second floor.

"You start at that end of the hall, I'll start here!" shouted Connel. "Smash everything you see!"

"Aye, aye, sir." Astro waved his hand and charged down the hall. He exploded into a room, firing rapidly, and an electronics engineer froze in a startled pose in front of his worktable. The big cadet gleefully swung a heavy chair across the table of delicate electronic instruments, and smashed shelves of vital parts, pausing only long enough to see if he had left anything unbroken. He rushed out into the hall again. At the other end he heard Connel in action in another room. Astro grinned. It sounded as if the major was having a good time. "Well," thought the big cadet, "I'm not having such a bad time myself!"

The next room he invaded contained the radar-control panel, and the big cadet howled with glee as he smashed the butt of his paralo-ray gun into the delicate vacuum tubes, and ripped wires and circuits loose.

Suddenly he stopped, conscious of someone behind him. He spun around, finger starting to squeeze the trigger of his gun, and then caught himself just in time. Major Connel was leaning against the doorjamb, a wide grin on his face.

"How're you doing?" he drawled.

"Not bad," said Astro casually. "Be a lot of work here, fixing these things, eh?" He grinned.

"What time is it?" asked Connel.

Astro looked at his watch. "Twenty to twelve."

"We'd better clear out of here and head for the jungle."

Astro hesitated. "You know, sir, I've been thinking."

"If you have an idea, spill it," said the major.

"How about releasing the prisoners, taking over a ship, and blasting off?"

"And have the Solar Guard fleet blast us out of the skies? No, sir! Come on, we've got to get moving!"

"We could still try to release Carson and the others," said Astro stoutly.

"We can try all right, but I don't think we'll be very successful."

The two spacemen returned to the first floor of the building and headed for the rear door without so much as a look at the line of frozen guards along the wall. Once outside, they skirted the edge of the building, staying close to the hedge, and then struck out boldly across the canyon floor toward the prison building. They were surprised to see that their smashing attack had gone unnoticed, and Connel reasoned that the constant roar of activity in the canyon had covered the sounds of their raid.

"We'll have to hurry, sir," said Astro as they turned into the lane leading to the prison. "Ten minutes to twelve."

"It's no good, Astro," said Connel, suddenly pulling the cadet back and pointing to the building. "Look at all the guards—at least a dozen of them."

Astro waited a second before saying grimly, "We could try, sir."

"Don't be a pigheaded idiot!" roared Connel. "Nothing will happen to those men now, and in five minutes there'll be so much confusion around here that we'll be able to walk over and open the door without firing a shot!"

Suddenly there was an explosive roar behind them and they spun around. On the opposite side of the canyon three rocket ships were hurtling spaceward.

"They must have spotted our fleet coming in," said Connel, a puzzled frown on his face.

"But how could they?" asked Astro. "We knocked out their radar!"

Connel slammed his fist into the palm of his hand. "By the stars, Astro, we forgot about their monitoring space-ship above the tower! When we knocked out the main station here in the canyon, it took over and warned the base of the attack!"

From all sides the canyon reverberated with the roaring blasts of the Nationalist fleet blasting off. Around them, the green-clad rebels were running to their defense posts. Officers shouted frantic orders and workers dropped tools to pick up guns. The building that held Carson and the other planters was suddenly left alone as the guards hurried to ships and battle stations.

Connel counted the number of ships blasting off and

smiled. "They don't stand a chance! They're sending up only two heavy cruisers, four destroyers, and about twenty scouts. The Solar Guard fleet will blast them into space dust."

Astro jumped up and started to run.

"Hey, Astro! Where are you going?" shouted Connel.

"To find Roger!" Astro shouted in reply. "I'll meet you back here!"

"Right!" shouted Connel, settling back into concealment. There was no need to release the planters in the guardhouse now. Connel was satisfied that in a few moments the rebellion against the Solar Alliance would be defeated. He smiled in prospect of seeing a good fight.

"BANDIT AT THREE O'CLOCK—RANGE TWENTY MILES!" Aboard the command ship of the first group of attacking Solar Guard squadrons, Captain Strong stood in the middle of the control deck and watched the outline of an approaching Nationalist cruiser on the radar scanner. The voice of the range finder droned over the ship's intercom.

"Change course three degrees starboard, one degree down on ecliptic plane," ordered Strong calmly.

"Aye, aye, sir," replied Tom at the controls.

"Main battery, stand by to fire." Strong watched the enemy ship closely.

"Aye, aye!" came the answer over the intercom.

"Approaching target!" called the range finder. "Closing to fifty thousand yards—forty thousand—"

"*Pleiades* and *Regulus*," Strong called the other two ships of his squadron. "Cut in on port and starboard flanks. Squadron B, stand by!"

Abrupt acknowledgment came over the audioceiver as the cruisers deployed for the attack.

"Twenty-three thousand yards, holding course." The range-finder's voice was a steady monotone.

"Stand by to fire!" snapped Strong.

"Two bandits at nine o'clock on level plane of ecliptic!" came the warning from the radar bridge.

Before Strong could issue an order countering the enemy move, the voice of the commander of the *Pleiades* came in over the audioceiver, "Our meat, Strong, you take care of the big baby!"

On the scanner screen Strong saw the trails of two space torpedoes erupt from the side of the *Pleiades*, followed immediately by two more from its flanking ship, the *Regulus*. The four missiles hurtled toward the two enemy destroyers, and a second later two brilliant flashes of light appeared on the scanner. Direct hits on the two destroyers!

"Range—ten thousand feet," came the calm voice over the intercom, reminding Strong of the enemy cruiser.

"Arm warheads!" snapped Strong over the intercom, and, on the gun deck, men twirled the delicate fuses on the noses of the space torpedoes and stepped back.

"On target!" called the range finder.

"Full salvo—fire!" called Strong, and turned to Tom quickly. "Ninety-degree turn—five degrees up!"

The Solar Guard cruiser quivered under the recoil of the salvo and then bucked under the sudden change of course to elude the torpedoes fired by the enemy a split second later.

As the Solar Guard cruiser roared up in a long arc, eluding the enemy torpedoes, the Nationalist ship maneuvered frantically to evade the salvo of war heads, but Strong had fired a deadly pattern. In a few seconds the enemy ship was reduced to space junk.

Concentrating on the control panel, Tom had been too busy maneuvering the giant ship to see the entire engagement, but he heard the loud exulting cries of the gun crew over the intercom. He looked up at Strong, and the Solar Guard captain winked. "One down!"

"Here come squadrons C, D, and E, sir," said Tom, indicating the radar. "Right on time." He glanced at the astral chronometer over his head. "Two minutes after twelve."

"It doesn't look as if we'll need them, Tom," said Strong. "The Nationalists got only two cruisers and four destroyers off the ground. We've already knocked out one of their cruisers and two destroyers, and Squadron B is taking on the second cruiser and its destroyer escorts now!" He turned to the radar scanner and saw the white evenly spaced blips that represented Squadron B enveloping the three enemy ships. The bulky converted cruiser was maneuvering frantically to get away. But there was no escape. In a perfectly coordinated action the Solar Guard ships fired their space torpedoes simultaneously. The three Nationalist ships exploded in a deadly flash of fire.

"Don't tell me that's all they've got!" exclaimed Strong. "Why, we still have the rest of the fleet coming in at 1205!"

Suddenly Tom froze in his seat. Before him on the radar scanner he saw a new cluster of white blips, seemingly coming from nowhere. They were enemy ships, hurtling spaceward to meet the Solar Guard fleet. "Captain Strong! Look! More of them. From secret ramps in the jungle!"

"By the craters of Luna!" roared the Solar Guard captain. "Attention! Attention! All ships—all ships!" he called into the fleet intercom. "This is Strong aboard command ship. Bandit formation closing fast. Regroup! Take tight defensive pattern!"

As the Solar Guard squadrons deployed to meet this new attack, Tom felt a chill run down his spine. The mass of ships blasting to meet them outnumbered them by almost three to one. And there were more ships blasting off from the secret ramps in the jungle! He had led the Solar Guard into a trap!

18

"FIRE AT WILL! FIRE AT WILL!"
Aboard the command ship, Captain Strong roared the order to the rest of the fleet, and the individual ship commanders of the Solar Guard vessels broke formation and rocketed into the mass of Nationalist ships, firing salvo after salvo of space torpedoes. But it was a losing battle. Time and again, Strong and Tom saw Solar

Guard ships hemmed in by three and four Nationalists' vessels, then blasted into oblivion.

Strong had ordered Tom to maneuver the command ship at will, seeking targets, yet still keeping from being a target, and the young cadet had guided the powerful ship through a series of maneuvers that had even surprised the experienced Solar Guard officer.

"Where's the rest of the fleet?" roared Strong. "Why aren't they here yet?"

"I don't know, sir," replied Tom, "but if they don't show up soon, there won't be much left to save!"

"Bandits dead ahead," droned the voice from the radar bridge calmly, "trying to envelop us."

Tom's hand shot out for the intercom to relay orders to the power deck and glanced quickly at the scanner. He almost cheered. "Steve—I mean, Captain Strong. The rest of the fleet! It's coming in! Attacking from topside!"

"By the craters of Luna, you're right!" yelled the young Solar Guard captain, as he saw the white blips on the scanner screen. "OK, it's time to stop running and fight!"

The Solar Guard reinforcements swooped down on the fighting ships with dazzling speed, and the sky over the jungle belt of Venus base was so thick with zooming, firing, maneuvering ships that observers on the ground couldn't tell one ship from another. For an hour the battle raged. During the seesawing back and forth it seemed as if all ships must be blasted into space junk. Finally the superior maneuvering and overall spacemanship of the Solar Guard vessels began to count heavily, and the Nationalist ships began to plunge into the jungle or drift helplessly out into space. Reforming, the Solar Guard ships encircled the enemy in a deadly englobement pattern, and wheeling in great coordinated arcs through space, sent combined volleys of torpedoes crashing into the enemy ships. The space battle was over, a complete Solar Guard victory.

Strong called to the remaining ships of his fleet, "Take formation K. Land and attack the enemy base according to prearranged order. The enemy fleet is destroyed, but we still have a big job to do."

"What happens now, sir?" asked Tom, relaxing for the

first time since the space battle had begun.

"We try to destroy their base and put an end to this rebellion as quickly as possible," replied Strong coldly.

One by one, the ships of the Solar Guard fleet landed around the rim of the canyon base. Troop carriers, that had stood off while the space battle raged, disgorged hundreds of tough Solar Guard Marines, each carrying shock rifles, paralo-ray pistols, and small narco grenades that would put an enemy to sleep in five seconds. A half-hour later, after the last Nationalist ship had been blasted out of the skies, the rim of the canyon was alive with Solar Guardsmen waiting to go into action. Many had comrades in the Solar Guard ships lost in the space fight and they were eager to avenge their friends.

"How many ships did we lose, sir?" asked Tom, after the squadron commanders had made their reports to Captain Strong.

"Forty," said Strong grimly. "But the entire Nationalist fleet was wiped out. Thank the universe that their radar was knocked out, or we would have been completely wiped out."

"Thank Astro and Major Connel for that, sir," said Tom with the first smile on his face in days. "I knew none of those green jokers could stop those two!"

"I've got to report to Commander Walters and the Solar Alliance, Tom. You take a squad of men and move out. Your job is to find Astro, Roger, and Major Connel."

"Thank you, sir!" said Tom happily.

DOWN IN THE CANYON, Major Connel had waited as long as he dared for Astro to return with news of Roger. From his position, the tough spaceman could not tell how the gigantic space battle had ended until he saw the Solar Guard troop carriers land on the rim of the canyon above. Satisfied, he decided that it was time to move.

He stood up, careful not to expose himself, since fighting had broken out among the workers. Every street, shop, and corner would bring dangers, and having stayed alive this far, Connel wanted to reach the Solar Guard forces and continue the fight alongside his friends. Astro was nowhere in sight when the major moved cautiously down a side alley, and he was beginning to think that Astro had not escaped from the base with Roger, when he saw the big cadet suddenly appear around a corner running as hard as he could. A few seconds later three green-clad Nationalist guards rounded the corner and pounded after him.

Astro saw Connel and ducked behind an overturned jet car, yelling, "I'm unarmed! Nail them, Major!"

In a flash Connel dropped to the pavement, and firing from a kneeling position, cut the Nationalists down expertly. When the last of the enemy was frozen, Connel rushed to Astro's side.

"What about Roger?" he asked.

"I couldn't reach him," replied Astro. "The sick bay's in the main administration building and that's so well guarded it would take a full company to break in."

Connel nodded grimly. "Well, the best thing for us to do is get more men and then tackle it."

"Yes, sir," said Astro. "I think we'd better head for the canyon walls on the west. The Marines are pouring down that side."

"Let's go," grunted the major, and led the way down the narrow lane. But when they reached the open area beyond the repair shops they saw that the Nationalist guards had thrown up barriers in the streets and were preparing defenses against frontal assault.

"Maybe we'd better stay where we are, sir," the big cadet said, after scanning the Nationalist defenses. "We'd never be able to get through now."

"Ummmh," mused Connel. "You're right. Maybe we can be of more use striking behind the lines."

Astro grinned. "That's just what I was thinking, sir." He pointed to a nearby barrier set up in the middle of the street. "We could pick off the men behind that—"

"Look out!" roared Connel. Behind them, five Nationalist guards had suddenly appeared. But they were more surprised than Astro and Connel, and the big cadet took advantage of it by charging right into them.

It was a short but vicious fight. There was no time to aim or fire a paralo-ray gun. It was a matter of bare knuckles and feet and knees and shoulders. One by one, the green-clad men were laid low, and finally, Connel, out of breath, turned to grin at Astro.

"Feel better," he gasped, "than I've felt in weeks!"

Astro grinned. One of Connel's front teeth was missing. Astro leaned against the wall and pointed to the canyon wall where the columns of Solar Guard Marines were making their way down into the base under heavy covering fire from above. "Won't be long now!"

"Come on," said Connel. "They'll probably send scouts out ahead of those columns and we can make contact with them over there." He pointed toward a high tangle of barbed wire set up in the middle of the nearby street. Astro nodded, and exchanging his broken ray gun for one belonging to a fallen Nationalist, raced to the edge of the barrier with the major. They crouched and waited for the first contact by the Marines.

"They shouldn't be too long now," said Connel.

"No more than a minute, sir," said Astro, pointing to a running figure darting from one protective position to another.

"You, there!" shouted a familiar voice. "Behind that barrier!"

Astro glanced at Connel. "Major, that sounds like—!"

"Come out with your hands in the air and nothing will happen to you!" the voice called again.

"By the stars, you're right!" yelled Connel. "It's Corbett!"

Astro jumped up and yelled, "Tom! Tom! You big space-brained jerk! It's me, Astro!"

Behind the corner of a house, Tom peered cautiously around the edge and saw the big cadet scramble over the tangle of barbed wire with Connel right behind him. Tom held up his hand for the squad in back of him to hold their fire and stepped out to meet his friends. "Major! Astro!"

The three spacemen pounded each other on the back while the patrol of Marines watched, grinning. "Where's Roger?" asked Tom finally.

Astro quickly told him of the heavily guarded administration building.

"Is he all right?" asked Tom.

"No one knows," replied Connel. "We haven't been able to get any news of him at all."

"I'm going after him," said Tom, his jaw set. "No telling what they'll try to do with him when they see their goose is cooked."

"I'll go with you," said Astro.

"No, you stay here with Major Connel," said Tom. "I think it would be better if just one tried it, with the rest creating a diversion on the other side."

"Good idea," said Connel. He turned to the rest of the patrol. "Men, there's an injured Space Cadet in the sick bay of the main building. He's the third member of the *Polaris* unit and has contributed as much to victory in this battle as any of us. We've got to get him out of the hands of the Nationalists before something happens to him. Are you willing to try?"

The Marines agreed without hesitation.

"All right," said Connel, "here's what we'll do." Quickly the major outlined a plan whereby Tom would sneak through the lines of the Nationalists around the administration building, while the rest of them created a diversionary move. It was a daring plan that would require split-second timing. When they were all agreed as to what they would do and the time of the operation was set, they moved off toward the administration building. The rebellion was over, defeated. Yet the Nationalist leaders were still alive. They were desperate men and Roger was in their hands. His life meant more to Tom Corbett and Astro than the smashing victory of the Solar Guard, and they were prepared to give their own lives to save his.

19

"READY?" ASKED CONNEL.
"ALL SET, SIR," REPLIED TOM.

"Remember, we'll open up in exactly five minutes and we'll continue to attack for another seven minutes. That's all the time you have to get inside, find Roger, and get out again."

"I understand, sir," replied Tom.

"Move out," said Connel, "and spaceman's luck!"

With a last quick glance at Astro who gave him a reassuring nod, Tom dropped to his knees and crawled out from behind their hidden position. Dropping flat on his stomach, he inched forward toward the administration building. All around him ray guns and blasters were firing with regularity as the columns of Marines advanced from all sides of the canyon toward the center, mopping up everything in front of them. The roof of the administration building seemed a solid sheet of fire as the Nationalist leaders fought back desperately.

He reached the side of the building that was windowless, and scrambled toward the back door without interference. There he saw five green-clad men, crouched behind sandbags, protecting the rear entrance. Glancing at his watch he saw the sweeping hand tick off the last few seconds of his allotted time. At the exact instant it hit the five-minute mark, there was a sudden burst of activity at the front of the building. Connel and the Marine patrol had opened fire in a mock attack. The men guarding the rear left their barricade and raced into the building to meet the new assault.

Without a second's hesitation, Tom jumped toward the door. He reached up, found it unlocked, and then with his ray-gun ready, kicked the door open. He rushed in and dived to the floor, ray-gun in his hand, ready to freeze anything or anyone in sight.

The hall was empty. In the front, the firing continued and the halls of the building echoed loudly with the frantic commands of the defenders. Gliding along the near wall, Tom moved slowly forward. Before him, a door was ajar and he eased toward it. On tiptoe the curly-haired cadet inched around the edge of the door and glanced inside. He saw a Nationalist guard on his hands and knees loading empty shock rifles. Tom quickly stepped inside and jammed his gun in the man's back. "Freeze!" he said between his teeth.

The trooper tensed, then relaxed, and slowly raised his hands.

"Where's the sick bay?" demanded Tom.

"On the second floor, at the end of the hall."

"Is that where you're keeping Cadet Manning?" demanded Tom.

"Yes," replied the man. "He's—"

Tom fired before the trooper could finish. It was rough, but he knew he had to act swiftly if he was to help Roger. The trooper was frozen in his kneeling position, and Tom scooped up a loaded shock rifle before slipping back into the hall. It was still empty. The firing outside seemed to be increasing.

He located the stairs, and after a quick but careful check, started up, heart pounding, guns ready. On the second floor he glanced up and down the hall, and jumped back into the stair well quickly. Firing from an open window, three troopers were between him and the only door at the end of the hall. Not sure if Roger was in that room or not, Tom had to make sure by looking. And the only way he could do that was to eliminate the men in his way. He dropped to one knee and took careful aim with the ray pistol. It would be tricky at such long range, but should the paralo-ray fail, the cadet was prepared to use the shock rifle. He fired, and for a breathless second waited for the effects of the ray on the troopers. Then he saw the men go rigid and he smiled. Three hundred feet with a ray pistol was very fancy shooting!

He raced for the door. As he entered the room, he saw a figure stretched out on the floor. He stopped still, cold fear clutching at his heart.

"Roger!" he called. The blond-haired cadet didn't move. Tom jumped to his unit mate's side and dropped to one knee beside him. It was dark in the room and he couldn't see very well, but there was no need for light when he felt Roger's pulse.

"Frozen, by the stars!" he exclaimed. He stepped back,

flipped the neutralizer switch on his ray-gun, and fired a short burst. Almost immediately Roger groaned, blinked his eyes, and sat up.

"Roger! Are you all right?" asked Tom.

"Yeah—sure. I'm OK," mumbled his unit mate. "Those dirty space rats. They didn't know what to do with me when the Marines landed, so they froze me. They were scared to kill me. Afraid of reprisals."

"They sure used their heads that time," said Tom with a grin. "How's your back?"

"Fine. I just wrenched it a little. It's better now. But never mind me. What's going on? Where's Astro and Major Connel? And how did you get here?"

Tom gave him a quick run-down on everything that had happened, concluding with, "Major Connel and Astro, with a patrol of Solar Guard Marines, are outside now drawing the Nationalist fire. Time's running out on us fast. Think you can walk?"

"Spaceboy," replied Roger, "to get out of this place I'd crawl on my hands and knees!"

"Then come on!" Tom gave the shock rifle to his unit mate and stepped back into the hall. It was quiet. Tom waved at Roger to follow and slipped down the hall toward the stairs. Outside, the Marine patrol continued firing, never letting up for a second. The two boys reached the stairs and had started down when Tom grabbed Roger by the arm. "There's someone moving around down there!"

They hugged the wall and held their breath. Tom glanced at his watch. Only forty-five seconds to go before the Marines would stop firing and retire. They had to get out of the building!

"We'll have to take a chance, Roger," murmured Tom. "We'll try to rush them and fight our way out."

"Don't bother!" said a harsh voice behind them. The two cadets spun around and looked back toward the second floor. Standing at the top of the stairs, Rex Sinclair scowled down at them, ray guns in each hand, leveled at the two cadets.

"By the craters of Luna!" cried Roger. "You!"

"That's one of the things I forgot to tell you, Roger,"

said Tom wryly. "Sinclair belongs to this outfit too!"

"Belongs?" roared Roger. "Look at that white uniform he's wearing! This yellow rat is Lactu, the head of the whole Nationalist movement!"

Tom gaped at the white-clad figure at the head of the stairs. "The leader!" he gasped.

"Quite right, Corbett," replied Sinclair quietly. "And if it hadn't been for three nosy cadets, I would have been the leader of the whole planet. But it's finished now. All that is left for me is escape. And you two are going to help me do just that!"

Roger suddenly dropped to one knee and leveled the blaster. But the Nationalist leader was too quick. His paralo-ray crackled and Roger was frozen solid.

"Why, you—!" roared Tom.

"Drop your gun, Corbett," warned Sinclair, "and take that blaster away from him."

"I'll get you, Sinclair," said Tom through clenched teeth, "and when I do—"

"Stop the talk and get busy!" snapped Sinclair.

Tom took the blaster out of Roger's paralyzed hands and dropped it on the floor. Still holding one ray-gun on Tom, Sinclair flipped on the neutralizer of the other gun and released Roger again.

"Now get moving down those stairs!" ordered Sinclair. "One more funny move out of either of you and I'll do more than just freeze you."

"What are you going to do with us?" asked Roger.

"As I said, you are going to help me escape. This time the Solar Guard has won. But there are other planets, other people who need strong leadership and who like to put on uniforms and play soldier. People will always find reason to rebel against authority, and I will be there to channel their frustrations into my own plans. Perhaps it will be Mars. Or Ganymede. Or even Titan. Another name, another plan, and once again the Solar Guard will have to fight me. Only next time, I assure you, it is I who will win!"

"There won't be any next time," growled Roger.

"You're washed up now. This base is swarming with Marines. How do you think you're going to get out of here?"

"You shall see, my friend. You shall see!"

Sinclair motioned them toward a door on the ground floor. "Open it!" demanded Sinclair. Tom opened it and stepped inside. It was a cleaner's closet, crammed with old-fashioned mops and pails and dirty rags. Sinclair pushed Roger inside and was about to follow when several green-clad guards came running down the hall toward them.

"Lactu! Lactu!" they shouted frantically. "They're pouring into the base! The Solar Guard—they've got us surrounded!"

"Keep fighting!" snapped Sinclair. "Don't surrender! Inflict as much damage as possible!"

"Where—where are you going?" asked one of the men, looking at the closet speculatively.

"Never mind me!" barked Sinclair. "Do as I tell you. Fight back!"

"It looks like we're losing a leader," observed another of the men slowly. "You wouldn't be running out on us, would you, Lactu?"

Sinclair fired three quick blasts from the ray-guns, freezing the men solid, and then turned back to Tom and Roger. "Stay in that closet and do as I tell you."

Inside the closet, Sinclair kicked a pail out of the way and barked, "Remove the loose plank in the floor and drop it on the floor."

Tom felt around until he found the loose board and lifted it up.

"What's down there?" asked Roger.

"You'll see," said Sinclair. "Now step back, both of you!"

Tom and Roger backed up and watched while Sinclair bent over the hole in the floor. He felt around inside with one hand and appeared to turn something. Suddenly the wall opposite the two cadets slid back to reveal a narrow flight of stairs leading down. Sinclair motioned with his gun again. "Get going, both of you."

Tom stepped forward, followed by Roger, and they started down the stairs. At the bottom they found themselves in a narrow tunnel about four hundred feet underground. The floor of the tunnel slanted downward sharply.

"At the end of this tunnel," announced Sinclair, "is a clearing and in that clearing is a spaceship. It is nearly three miles from the canyon. By the time the Solar Guard learns of my absence, we shall be lost in space."

"We?" asked Tom. "You're taking us with you?"

"But of course," said Sinclair. "How else would I assure myself that the Solar Guard will not harm me unless I take two of their most honored Space Cadets with me?"

"IT'S BEEN FIFTEEN MINUTES," announced Connel, "and they haven't come out yet. There's only one thing to do. Take that building and find out what's happened."

The major was crouched behind a wrecked jet car, staring at the administration building.

"I can get that Marine captain over to our left to coordinate an attack with us, sir," suggested Astro.

"It's risky," said Connel. "They still have a lot of men in there. But if we wait for another column to reach us, it might be too late. All right, Astro, tell him we're attacking in ten minutes and ask him to give us all the help he can."

"Yes, sir," replied Astro, and flopped to the ground to worm his way toward the head of the Marine column on the left.

It took the cadet nearly five minutes to cover the hundred yards between the two Solar Guard positions. Several times the firing became so heavy that the cadet was forced to remain still on the ground while rifle and ray-gun fire crackled over his head. He made it finally, several Marines coming out to help him over the top of the barrier. Gasping for breath, the big cadet asked to see the commanding officer.

A grimy, tired-looking officer turned and walked over to the cadet.

"Astro!"

"Captain Strong!"

"Where's Tom and Roger and Major Connel?" demanded Strong.

Astro told the captain of Tom's attempt to save Roger and that nothing had been heard from him since. "Major Connel wants us to attack together," Astro continued. "He's jumping off in four minutes!"

"Right!" snapped Strong. He turned to a young Solar Guard officer waiting respectfully nearby. "You take them in, Ferris. Full frontal attack. Don't use blasters unless you have to. Take as many prisoners as possible."

"Very well, sir," replied the lieutenant.

"I'll go back to the other position with Cadet Astro. Start your attack as soon as you see Major Connel and his men go in."

"Got it, sir," said the lieutenant.

Strong and Astro made their way back to Connel's position quickly, and after a brief but hearty handclasp, the two officers began plotting the last assault against the Nationalists' stronghold. While other Marine columns were wiping up small groups of rebels fighting from disabled spaceships, repair shops, and other buildings, Strong's column had been driving straight for the heart of the base. The administration building was the last barrier between them and complete victory over the rebels.

Strong and Connel spoke briefly of Tom and Roger, neither wanting to voice his inner fears in front of Astro. The Nationalists previously had shown little regard for human life. Now, with their backs to the wall, Connel and Strong knew that if Tom and Roger were captured, they might be used as hostages to ensure safe passage for some of the rebels.

"Let's go," said Connel finally. "Tom and Roger will be expecting us." He forced himself to grin at Astro, but the giant cadet turned and faced the building grimly. Connel lifted his hand, took a last look up and down the line of waiting Marines, then brought his hand down quickly. "Over the top. Spaceman's luck!" he shouted.

The Marines vaulted over the top of their defense position and charged madly toward the building, all guns blazing. The Nationalists returned the fire, and for the first few seconds it seemed that the world had suddenly gone mad. Strong found himself shouting, running, and firing in a red haze. Astro was roaring at the top of his lungs, and Connel just charged ahead blindly. Marines began to drop on all sides, cut down by the withering fire. Then, when it appeared that they would have to fall back, the main column, led by the Solar Guard lieutenant, broke through the last barricade and swarmed into the building.

Five minutes later the battle was over. The last remnants of the Nationalists had been defeated and the green-clad troopers were herded into the streets like cattle. Strong and Connel, followed by Astro, charged through the building like wild bulls searching for Tom and Roger.

"No sign of them," said Strong finally. "They must have slipped out somehow."

"No!" roared Connel. "They've been taken out of here as hostages. I'll bet my life on that. There must be a secret way out of here!"

"Come on," said Strong. "Let's find it." Suddenly he stopped. "Look! Those three troopers outside that door! They're frozen! Let's have a look there first!"

They rushed over to the closet where the three Nationalists had been frozen by Sinclair.

Strong stopped and gasped. "By the craters of Luna, it's Sharkey!"

"Sharkey? Who's that?" asked Astro.

"Supposed to be the leader of the Nationalists," said Connel.

Strong quickly released Sharkey from the paralo-ray effects and the man shuddered so violently from the reaction that Astro had to grab him to keep him from falling down.

"Where are Corbett and Manning?" demanded Connel.

"Lactu ... he took them both in there ... through a secret passageway." Sharkey pointed to the closet with a trembling finger.

Strong jumped for the closet door and jerked it open. He saw the open wall and the stairs leading down. "Come on! This way!"

Connel ran wildly into the closet, followed by Astro. Suddenly the big cadet stopped, turned, and fired point-blank at the figurehead of the Nationalist rebellion. Sharkey once again grew rigid.

The two Solar Guard officers raced down the stairs into the tunnel and ran headlong through the darkness. Time was precious now. The lives of Tom and Roger might be lost by a wasted second.

20 "WHAT'S THAT NOISE, TOM?" The two cadets were walking through the tunnel when they heard the strange booming roar. Behind them, Sinclair overheard Roger's whispered question and laughed. "That is the sound of the slaves being fed their lunch. They do not know yet that there has been a battle and soon they'll be free!"

"Slaves!" gasped Roger. "What kind of slaves?"

"You shall see. Keep going!" Sinclair prodded the cadets with his ray-gun. The tunnel had grown larger and the downward slant of the floor lessened as they pressed forward. The noise ahead of them grew louder and stronger and now they could distinguish occasional words above the din.

"We must pass through the big vault where the slaves are working," said Sinclair. "I would advise you to keep your mouths shut and do as I say!"

Neither Tom nor Roger answered, keeping their eyes straight ahead.

The tunnel suddenly cut sharply to the right and they could see a blaze of light in front of them. The two boys stopped involuntarily, and then were nudged forward by Sinclair's guns. Before them was a huge cavern nearly a thousand yards high and three thousand yards across, illuminated by hundreds of torches. Along one side of the cave a line of men were waiting to have battered tin plates filled from a huge pot at the head of the line. The men were in rags, and every one of them was hardly more than skin and bones. At strategic places around the cavern, Nationalist guards kept their guns trained and ready to fire. They brought up their guns quickly as Tom and Roger entered, and then lowered them again as Sinclair appeared. Every eye turned to the Nationalist leader as he marched across the floor of the cave, Tom and Roger walking before him.

"You see," said Sinclair, "these wretched fools thought my organization was a utopia until they learned that I was no better for them than the Solar Guard. Unfortunately they learned too late and were sent here to dig underground pits for my spaceships and storage dumps."

The small column of three marched across the floor of the cave toward another small tunnel on the opposite side. The slaves were absolutely still, and the guards smiled a greeting at their leader when he passed them.

Sinclair ignored them all. "Beyond that tunnel," he continued, pointing to the small opening ahead of them, "there is a spaceship. We will board that ship and blast off. The three of us. Where we will go, I haven't decided yet. Perhaps a long trip into deep space until the Solar Guard has forgotten about you and me and the Nationalists. Then we will return, as I said before, to Mars, or perhaps Ganymede, and I will start all over again."

"You're mad!" said Tom through clenched teeth. "Crazy as a space bug!"

"We shall see, Corbett. We shall see!"

Suddenly Roger broke away and raced toward the mass of slaves. He shouted wildly, "Get the guards! The Nationalists are beaten! The base in the canyon has been destroyed! Hurry! Rebel!"

The emaciated men milled around the cadet, all asking questions at once.

Sinclair signaled to the guards. "Shoot him down!" Four guards took careful aim.

"Roger! Look out!" warned Tom.

Roger whirled around in time to see the guards about to fire. He dived for a mound of dirt and hid behind it. The energy shock waves licked at the sand where he had stood a second before. Roger got up and ran for better cover, the guards continuing to fire at him. Then, around the cadet, the slave workers began to come alive. Some hurled stones at the guards, others began climbing up the sides to the ledges where the guards stood. Taking in the situation at a glance, Sinclair shoved the ray gun in Tom's back and snarled, "Get going!"

The young cadet had no alternative. He turned and marched hurriedly across the floor toward the small tunnel ahead of him. Several slave workers tried to attack Sinclair, but in their weakened condition, they were no match for the alert Nationalist leader who froze them instantly with his paralo-ray gun.

Roger saw Tom heading for the tunnel and made a sudden dash for Sinclair. But the rebel leader heard the pounding of footsteps and turned to fire at Roger as the cadet sailed through the air in a flying tackle. The jolting ray hit him squarely and he landed on the ground with a thud a few feet from Sinclair, completely immobilized again.

Tom tried to seize the momentary advantage, but once again Sinclair was quicker and forced Tom back into the small opening of the tunnel.

Around them, the slave workers were being whipped into a frenzy after months of stored-up hatred for their guards. Hundreds of them were climbing up toward the guards' posts, unmindful of the deadly fire pouring down on them.

"Get in there quick!" demanded Sinclair. He shoved Tom through the small opening, and after a quick glance over his shoulder at the surging slaves, followed the cadet.

Sinclair flashed a light ahead of them and Tom saw the reflection of a bright surface. In the distance he recognized the outlines of a spaceship.

"Keep moving!" ordered Sinclair. "You're my protection in getting out of here, and if I have to freeze you and carry you aboard, that's just what I'll do! Now get moving!"

Tom walked to the airlock of the ship, Sinclair right in back of him. The rebel leader pressed an outside button in the ship's stabilizer fin and the port swung open slowly. "Get in!" growled Sinclair.

Tom stepped into the ship and waited. Sinclair climbed in in back of him and closed the airlock.

"Through that hatch," said Sinclair, motioning toward the iron ladder, "and keep your hands in the air."

"How do you think you're going to get through the Solar

Guard fleet that's standing off above the canyon?" asked Tom casually. "As soon as they see this ship blast off, you'll have a hundred atomic war heads blasting after you!"

"Not as long as I have you!" sneered Sinclair. "You're my protection!"

"You're wrong," said Tom. "They'll open fire, anyway."

"That's the chance I've got to take," said Sinclair. "Now climb up to the control deck and get on the audioceiver. You're going to tell them you're aboard!"

Tom walked ahead of the rebel leader toward the control deck, his mind racing. He knew that Sinclair was going through with his plan and he also knew that the Solar Guard would not pay any attention to anything he had to say. If, after three warnings, Sinclair didn't brake jets and bring his ship to a stop, he would be blasted out of space. He had to do something.

"Where's the communicator?" asked Tom.

"Over by the radar scanner." Sinclair eyed him suspiciously. "Remember, Corbett, your life depends on this as much as mine. If you don't convince them you're worth saving by letting me get away, you're a dead pigeon!"

"You don't have to tell me," said Tom. "I know when I'm licked."

Sinclair took his position in the pilot's chair, facing the control panel. For a brief moment his back was to Tom as he bent over to turn on the generators. Tom took a deep breath and lurched across the deck. But Sinclair turned and saw him coming, and jerked up the ray-gun. He wasn't able to get clear in time. Tom's fingers circled the barrel of the gun as Sinclair fired.

The barrel grew hot as Sinclair fired repeatedly. Tom's fingers were beginning to blister under the intense heat, but he held on. With his other hand he reached up for the rebel's throat. Sinclair grabbed his wrist and, locked together, they rolled around on the deck.

Sinclair continued to fire the ray gun and Tom's fingers were burning with pain from the heat. Suddenly the cadet let go the gun, spun around, and jerked Sinclair off balance. He swung his free hand as hard as he could into the rebel's stomach. Sinclair doubled over and staggered back, dropping the gun. Tom was on top of him like a shot, pounding straight, jolting rights and lefts to the man's head and stomach. But Sinclair was tough. He twisted around, and quick as a cat, jumped to his feet. Then, stepping in, he rapped a solid right to Tom's jaw. The cadet reeled back, nearly falling to the deck. Sinclair was in on top of him in a flash, pounding his head and body with vicious smashing blows.

Tom fell to the floor under the savagery of the rebel leader's attack. Sinclair lifted his foot to kick the cadet as Tom's fingers tightened around the barrel of the discarded ray gun. He brought it up sharply against the planter's shin and he staggered back in pain. Tom took careful aim. He fired the gun. Nothing happened. The gun was empty.

Sinclair rushed the cadet again, but Tom stepped aside and swung the heavy gun with all his might. The metal smashed against Sinclair's head and he sank to the deck, out cold.

The last rebel of Venus had been defeated.

"WE FOUND ROGER trying to keep the slaves away from the guards," said Strong. "They were ready to tear them apart!"

"Can't say that I blame them," snorted Connel. "Some of those poor devils had been working in the caves for three years!"

Tom, Roger, and Astro sat sprawled in chairs in one of the offices of the Nationalist headquarters listening to Strong and Major Connel sum up the day's battle. The entire army of Nationalist guards, Division Chiefs, and workers had been rounded up and put aboard the troop carriers to be taken to a prison asteroid. Each individual rebel would be dealt with under special court proceedings to be established by Solar Alliance decree later.

"There are still some things I don't understand," said Astro. "How did they know you were going to investigate them in the first place?"

"After our meeting with Commander Walters," said Connel, "we sent a special coded message to the Solar Alliance Delegate here on Venus. His secretary intercepted the message, used stolen priorities for himself and two assistants to get to Earth and back on an express space liner without being missed."

"The secretary!" shouted Tom. "That's the same fellow I saw in Atom City when we were bumped out of our seats on the *Venus Lark*!"

Roger looked up at Tom with a scowl. "A fine time to remember!"

Strong grinned. "We discovered him, Tom, when that attempt was made to kidnap you by the cab driver. We also picked up the owner of the pawnshop."

"The most amazing thing about this space joker, Sinclair," commented Connel, "was the way he had everyone fooled. I couldn't figure out how he was able to get around so quickly until I learned about those buildings."

"What buildings?" asked Tom, suddenly remembering how the rebel leader had disappeared so quickly and quietly when he was being held captive with Mr. and Mrs. Hill in the Sinclair home.

"Every one of the important members of the organization, the Division Chiefs, they called themselves, had a small shack on his property near the edge of the jungle. It was nothing more than a covering for a shaft that led to a tunnel, which, in turn, led to other tunnels under the jungle and eventually connected with one leading right into the base."

"You mean," said Astro, "they have underground tunnels all through the jungle?"

"That's right," asserted Connel. "If they had been prepared for our attack, they could have beaten the pants off us. Not only in space, but on the ground. They could have run circles around us in those tunnels. I got suspicious when I found a hut at the Sharkey place with no windows in it."

"Say, remember the time Sinclair barked at me for going near that shack on his place when we first arrived?" said Roger.

Connel grinned. "I'll bet you a plugged credit that if you had opened that door you'd have been frozen stiffer than a snowman on Pluto."

"Well, anyhow," said Tom happily, "we got what we came after."

"What was that?" asked Strong.

"A tyrannosaurus!" replied the curly-haired cadet.

"And that's another thing," said Connel. "That tyranno-saurus we killed was a pet of the Nationalists. I don't mean a household pet, but it fitted into their plans nicely. The tyranno's lair was near the top of that canyon. Any time a stray hunter came along, the tyrannosaurus would scare him away. So when you three came along and said you were deliberately hunting for a tyrannosaurus, they got worried."

"Worried?" asked Roger. "Why?"

"They thought you were actually hunting or investigat-ing them, and when I started nosing around, they were sure. That's why Sinclair ordered his boys to burn down his plantation—to try to throw us off the track. So you see," Connel concluded, "your summer leave really started the ball rolling against them."

"Summer leave!" shouted Roger. "What day is it?"

"The twenty-ninth of August," replied Strong.

"Oh, no!" moaned the blond-haired cadet. "We start back to class in three days!"

"Three days!" roared Astro. "But—but it'll take three days to write up our reports of everything that's happened! We won't have any time for fun!"

"Fun!" snorted Connel. "Fun is for little boys. **YOU THREE SPACE-BRAINED, ROCKET-HEADED IDIOTS ARE SPACEMEN!**"

★ ★ ★ ★ ★

TOM CORBETT WILL RETURN—
IN **TREACHERY**
IN OUTER SPACE

You might also enjoy:

DIET FOR DREAMERS:

Inspiration to Feed Your Dreams, Encouragement to Foster Your Creativity   ISBN: 978-0-9796335-7-7

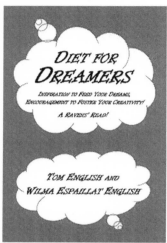

Five dozen witty and inspiring articles highlighting everything from Sherlock Holmes to Slinky toys, Stan Lee to Lucille Ball, the Monkees to Mother's Day, Hersey chocolate to Julia Child, and much much more; plus handling fear, rejection and failure.

Everyone has a special dream. Whether you're an artist or a writer, an actor or a singer, an inventor or an entrepreneur; or simply someone who dreams of better days ahead, Tom and Wilma English want to help you achieve your goals, by encouraging you to faithfully pursue your dreams while providing you with practical advice and inspiring stories. In this collection you'll discover fascinating facts and a few humorous turns about men and women, young and old, who dreamed big and succeeded despite shaky circumstances, overwhelming obstacles and, often, the silly notions of our wonderful, whacky world. **$7.95**

Made in the USA
Middletown, DE
23 November 2018